You're invited to…

Return to Tyler

Where scandals and secrets
are unleashed in a small town
and love is found around every corner…

Don't miss any of these
wonderful love stories!

Dear Reader,

November is an exciting month here at Harlequin American Romance. You'll notice we have a brand-new look—but, of course, you can still count on Harlequin American Romance to bring you four terrific love stories sure to warm your heart.

Back by popular demand, Harlequin American Romance revisits the beloved town of Tyler, Wisconsin, in the RETURN TO TYLER series. Scandals, secrets and romances abound in this small town with fabulous stories written by some of your favorite authors. The always wonderful Jule McBride inaugurates this special four-book series with *Secret Baby Spencer*.

Bestselling author Muriel Jensen reprises her heartwarming WHO'S THE DADDY? series with *Father Fever*. Next, a former wallflower finally gets the attention of her high school crush when he returns to town and her friends give her a makeover and some special advice in *Catching His Eye*, the premiere of Jo Leigh's THE GIRLFRIENDS' GUIDE TO... continuing series. Finally, Harlequin American Romance's theme promotion, HAPPILY WEDDED AFTER, which focuses on marriages of convenience, continues with Pamela Bauer's *The Marriage Portrait*.

Enjoy them all—and don't forget to come back again next month when another installment in the RETURN TO TYLER series from Judy Christenberry is waiting for you.

Wishing you happy reading,

Melissa Jeglinski
Associate Senior Editor
Harlequin American Romance

SECRET BABY SPENCER

Jule McBride

HARLEQUIN®

TORONTO • NEW YORK • LONDON
AMSTERDAM • PARIS • SYDNEY • HAMBURG
STOCKHOLM • ATHENS • TOKYO • MILAN • MADRID
PRAGUE • WARSAW • BUDAPEST • AUCKLAND

Special thanks and acknowledgment are given to
Jule McBride for her contribution to
the Return To Tyler series.

ISBN 0-373-16849-7

SECRET BABY SPENCER

ABOUT THE AUTHOR

In 1993 Jule McBride's dream came true with the publication of her debut novel, *Wild Card Wedding*. It received the *Romantic Times* Reviewer's Choice Award for Best First Series Romance. Ever since, the author has continued to pen stories that have met with strong reviews and made repeated appearances on romance bestseller lists.

Books by Jule McBride

HARLEQUIN AMERICAN ROMANCE

*Big Apple Babies
**The Little Matchmaker

HARLEQUIN INTRIGUE

Don't miss any of our special offers. Write to us at the following address for information on our newest releases.

Harlequin Reader Service
U.S.: 3010 Walden Ave., P.O. Box 1325, Buffalo, NY 14269
Canadian: P.O. Box 609, Fort Erie, Ont. L2A 5X3

Who's Who in Tyler

Seth Spencer—There's a wealth of passion burning beneath this banker's three-piece suit!

Jenna Robinson—She's got a bridal gown in tow— and a baby on the way....

Quinn and Brady Spencer—Seth's sexy brothers. Their motto is: "No Spencer man ever commits!"

Elias Spencer—His wife ran away with his heart....

Martha Bauer, Bea Ferguson, Emma Finklebaum, Merry Linton, Tillie Phelps—The famous Quilting Circle—their quilts are the very fabric of Tyler.

Caroline Benning—the waitress is new to town, and not too sure if she'll stay....

Johnny and Anna Kelsey—Their boardinghouse is Home Sweet Home—for them and their guests.

Rev. Sarah Baron—Everyone in town is part of her flock.

Tillie Olsen—At her beauty salon, customers get the latest hairstyles—and the hottest gossip!

Chapter One

A town away, in Belton's substation, police captain Brick Bauer was the first to frown, rise from his desk and walk to the window. "Probably kids," he decided, glaring at the winking, cat-eyed taillights of a suspicious-looking dented gold Cadillac heading toward Tyler, Wisconsin. "No adult around here drives a car that sounds like...like..." Brick shook his head, his mind unable to seize upon any suitable phrase.

"Like the end of the world," Reverend Sarah Baron said decisively a few minutes later, looking up from her desk in the Tyler Fellowship Sanctuary. Vaguely, Sarah wondered if the car would wind up stopping in town and if the passenger was feeling friendless and lonely or might someday become a member of her parish, then she said, "Maybe Michael can do something about that awful-sounding muffler." Yes, if the driver couldn't afford a mechanic, surely Sarah's husband would offer to look at the car free of charge, though by the sound of it, even an act of God wouldn't fix it. "Oh ye of little faith," Sarah sighed after a few moments, still chiding herself as, some distance away, Martha Bauer gaped through the window of a stately brick Victorian known as Worthington House, then at the ladies seated around a quilting frame.

"Look at that woman's hair!" exclaimed Martha with a gasp.

Pausing, needles raised in midair, the other women, mostly elderly, stared curiously through the window into the twilight, scrutinizing the Cadillac sedan idling at the new stop sign on the corner. The driver had short, spiky dark brown hair, streaked with red. "Her hairstyle's certainly inventive," Lydia Perry remarked, knowing nothing less could have drawn her mind from the date she'd shared last night with Elias Spencer.

"And is that a wedding dress bunched in the passenger seat?" asked Martha, squinting.

"Sure looks like it," said Bea Ferguson, determined to speak before anyone initiated another argument about whether or not the new stop sign was really necessary. "And look. She's got a baby in the back. I see a car seat."

"A baby?" Lydia leaned forward, wondering where the woman was headed and whether there was a man in the picture. "Do you all think that poor woman's running from some kind of trouble?"

"Who knows?" sighed Bea. "But if she stops in town for the night, she'll probably head for the Kelsey Boarding House or the Timberlake Lodge, which means we'll hear the gossip if there is any."

"Or she'll go to Granny Rose's," Martha added,

referring to Tyler's bed-and-breakfast. "It's just a good thing she didn't park in front of Worthington House. That car looks like something bequeathed by Elvis, don't you think?" she continued as she bent her head over the quilting frame and surveyed the fabric with sharp eyes that belied her eighty-seven years. "I'd rather walk a mile in orthopedic shoes than be caught dead in a car as awful as that."

"Martha, not everybody can afford a late-model car," Kaitlin Rodier reminded gently. The newest group member glanced up from the patchwork quilt. "Besides," she chided, "with hair like that, she's got to be from a city, and let's face it, Tyler can always use some new blood, even if she's just passing through."

"City people," grunted Tillie Phelps grumpily, cocking her head and taking in the quilt's royal blue border. "I figure we've got enough excitement with Quinn Spencer stopping by to chat with us all the time, and with that woman, Caroline Benning, coming to town."

Everyone fell silent, considering the new waitress at Marge's Diner. The young woman's stay at the Kelsey Boarding House had been uneventful, but just last week she'd been found tangled in the rose bushes outside Elias Spencer's house. She'd sworn she was chasing a stray cat she wanted to take to a vet, but no cat was ever found and now most people figured she'd been spying on the Spencers.

"Well," Bea finally said as she continued stitching one of the group's sought-after quilts that were so popular around Tyler, "in addition to Caroline Benning's being here, all the Spencer boys have come home. Caroline was probably trying to peek at Quinn through the window of Elias's place, don't you think?"

"Probably," Martha agreed. "Quinn *is* awfully cute."

"All those Spencer boys are good looking," Emma Finklebaum mused, nodding as the Cadillac lurched past the stop sign, into the intersection. "Hey, what if that woman knows the Spencers? She *does* look like she's from a city, and the Spencers came from New York, remember?"

"Who could forget?" murmured Martha, and for a moment the quilting circle fell respectfully silent again since no one intended to discuss the scandal that had followed the Spencer family to Tyler twenty-three years ago.

"Poor boys," Lydia finally said, thinking of how her new beau, Elias, had brought his New York society family here to start a life years ago—only to have his wife run off with her New York lover. Lydia and Elias had only been on a few dates, but Lydia liked him and was beginning to fear he wouldn't learn to love again, no more than his sons probably would.

"Tragic, what Violet Spencer's leaving Tyler did to those boys," Emma continued in a hushed, sympathetic tone. "Seth was the oldest, but he was only fourteen at the time. Of course they're not boys anymore, they're full-grown men, but you can bet none of them will ever trust a woman."

"Much less marry one," Martha agreed with a sad sigh as the gold Cadillac vanished from sight, pulling into Tyler proper and around the town square, prompting a worried Cooper Night Hawk to stare from inside the police station, instinctively double-checking for his gun and badge.

"Ten to one, there's no current inspection on a vehicle that sounds as bad as that," Cooper muttered in disgust. At least the driver was a woman, which meant she wasn't the armed male felon Cooper had just heard about on the dispatch radio. Cooper continued staring through the window, running a hand through his long dark hair, his dark eyes narrowing. Even without seeing the license plate, he now recognized the Cadillac as registered to the rent-a-wreck business at the Madison airport. Whoever the stranger was, she'd flown into Wisconsin.

Sighing, Cooper watched the car continue around the town square. It was dark outside, the gunmetal gray, late October sky both windy and carrying the first whipping sting of winter. As the car passed under a streetlamp, the interior was illuminated and Cooper's hawklike eyes made out the driver's delicate features. Striking, he decided. She had a birdlike face with a thin, straight nose and sculpted cheekbones; the artfully cut, jagged ends of her jaw-length hair spiked against a creamy jaw, then feathered down, sweeping her neck. She was a volcano, he decided. Secretly seething and possibly volatile, at least according to his sixth sense. "But what's a woman who looks like that doing here?" Tyler was hardly a hub.

And she wasn't alone, either. She had a baby in the back seat.

Whatever the case, she and the baby weren't posing any threat to Tyler's peace, so the lawman finally turned toward his desk, just as Nora Gates Forrester glanced through the windows of her department store. She'd been rearranging a Halloween display, and as she gawked at the out-of-place gold Cadillac, her well-manicured hand continued fluffing the green wig atop a mannequin dressed as a witch. "I bet that's a friend of those Spencer boys," Nora murmured on a premonition as the car rounded the tree-filled square, passing the town hall, dry cleaners and drug store. "Or maybe not," Nora amended, frowning when the sedan didn't stop at the corner, or in front of the Spencer-owned bank, the Tyler Savings & Loan, but instead continued toward The Hair Affair, where Marge Phelps, owner of Tyler's favorite eatery, Marge's Diner, popped her head out from under a hair dryer. "Now there's a hairstyle," she declared, peering through the window at the passing car. "Get a gander, everybody."

"Your daughter's acting on Broadway in New York," chided Sandy Stirling who'd come in for a trim after leaving her job at the town's most successful homegrown business, Yes! Yogurt. "And you go to New York all the time, Marge. You, of all people, should be used to seeing weird hair."

"Maybe, but there's a wedding dress and a baby in the back seat of that car," countered Marge.

"A baby? Oh, good! For a minute, I was worried,"

confessed Molly Blake who, despite the expense, had run in to get her nails done. "I thought it might be that artist…you know, that friend of Seth Spencer's who agreed to come to town to design the logo, invitations and menus for the bed-and-breakfast I want to open. She said she wouldn't be here until tomorrow, so I'm not ready to meet her, but if that woman's got a baby…"

"Then it can't be her," finished Tisha, who owned The Hair Affair. "That artist—uh, Jenna Robinson's her name, right?—she didn't say she had a baby, did she, Molly?"

Molly swallowed hard. "No, but now that I think about it, I guess she might. How would I know?" Molly still couldn't decide what to make of the call she'd received from Jenna, who'd introduced herself as an old friend of Seth Spencer's. Molly had figured she was in luck. If a good friend of the local bankers was designing the menus for the bed-and-breakfast Molly wanted to open, he'd be more likely to give Molly a loan, wouldn't he? Still, why would an artist call Molly all the way from New York, offer to pay her own traveling expenses to Wisconsin, then agree to do the artwork so cheaply? Even more suspiciously, Jenna had made Molly swear not to tell Seth Spencer she was coming to town, saying she wanted to surprise him.

Dear Lord…what if the woman in the Cadillac is Jenna Robinson? What if she's come to Tyler with a baby of Seth Spencer's…a baby Seth doesn't even know exists?

There goes my loan.

Molly squelched the thought. Yes, she'd definitely started reading too much romance fiction in the lonely times after her husband died. In real life, women didn't putter into small, uneventful towns like Tyler, driving old gold Cadillacs and wielding babies they'd kept secret from banker daddies. Frowning, Molly stared down at her drying, passion-pink nails, trying to assure herself that tomorrow's interview with Seth Spencer would go well. Surely, her uneasiness about Jenna's arrival was unfounded. As soon as possible, maybe even tomorrow, Jenna and Seth would be jointly surveying Molly's Victorian home. On the phone, Jenna had been responsive to Molly's ideas for transforming the place into a romantic hideaway; now Molly was hoping Jenna's artistic excitement would help convince Seth to fork over the start-up capital.

No, Molly decided with finality, the wild-looking woman in the Cadillac with the wedding dress and baby couldn't be Jenna Robinson. Fate simply wasn't that unkind. Nevertheless, Molly was still exhaling a worried sigh as the car halted, idling outside Eden Frazier's flower shop, The Garden of Eden. Inside, Eden brushed back her brown hair, lifted a watering can and stepped around a bucket of eucalyptus. As she inhaled the deep, sweet scent of some nearby roses, her violet eyes squinted, taking in the ancient gold tank. A whimsical smile stretched her lips when she saw the wild-looking woman inside the car who was staring toward the Savings & Loan. "Where did *she* come from?" Eden whispered.

"New York City," muttered the only resident of Tyler who could accurately answer that question. Seth Spencer watched the car and driver from his office in the bank. "But what for?"

Me.

"Seth," he growled, "that's not Jenna."

But ever since he'd left New York, Seth had been glimpsing Jenna everywhere: in the Alberta Ingalls Memorial Library, in Amanda Baron Trask's law offices, outside Marge's Diner. The woman never really was Jenna, of course. Never would be, either. Jenna's feelings—or lack of them—were clear when Seth calmly left her Soho loft six weeks ago.

No, the woman in the gold Cadillac couldn't be Jenna.

Seth glanced past Molly Blake's loan proposal and today's copy of the *Tyler Citizen,* both of which were on his desk, then around the bank's homey, old-fashioned interior, taking in the red-carpeted floors leading to the teller area. Maybe he should at least head into the lobby and check out the car...

Seth, it's not her!

Fighting the urge to reach behind him and grab the gray wool jacket to his suit, he swallowed hard, denying his emotions. He shifted his oxford-clad feet, then started to take an unlit cigar out of his mouth and tighten the silver Hermés tie around the collar of his white-pressed shirt. But he didn't move. *Even if it is her, which it's not, let her come to me.*

That was more his style. He'd never let a woman, especially Jenna, see him come running. The house he'd foolishly bought near his father's Victorian on Maple Street flashed through his mind, and he damned Jenna again, now for how unhappy he'd felt living there these past six weeks. One too many times, he'd found himself standing in the foyer, staring down the block, taking in the wraparound porch and gingerbread trim of his father's house, a place that had lost its womanly touch after Seth's mother, Violet, ran off with a man named Ray Bennedict when Seth was fourteen.

Too late Seth had realized that the last thing he needed was to own a four-bedroom house on the same block where he'd grown up. "Too much history," he muttered now. The sparse steel furniture he'd brought from Manhattan barely filled the living room, and when Seth crossed the hardwood floors, his echoing footsteps sounded empty and hollow, evoking exactly what he'd felt when his mother vanished from Tyler.

He blew out an angry sigh. He should have known Jenna wouldn't stick around, no more than his mother had. Even worse, before his return to Tyler, he hadn't thought about his mother for years. In New York, he'd always flown high on external stimulus, his blood rushing with the sound of car horns or ticker tape announcing the latest hot deal on Wall Street. But six weeks ago Seth had landed in Tyler again, harboring still-raw feelings he hadn't noticed for years. Which was why he needed to quit imagining

Jenna was in town. Just like his mother, Jenna had proven she didn't give a damn.

"Get over it," he muttered, reaching for the phone. He'd been expecting one of his brothers, Quinn or Brady, to call before quitting time to see if he wanted to get supper at Marge's Diner, but now Seth thought maybe he should take the initiative for once and call them. But no, somewhere along the line, he'd learned to watch and wait, to gauge how much others extended themselves while holding his own cards close to the vest. Whether the lesson had come from his mother's abandonment or from working in New York's cutthroat financial industry, Seth wasn't sure. Either way, he wound up not picking up the phone.

The whole time, his liquid brown eyes stayed riveted on the Cadillac idling in front of Eden's flower shop. Outwardly, he didn't move a muscle; inwardly, he was going crazy. From here, the woman *did* look like Jenna. For a second, he pretended it was, and that she was impressed by the one-story brick Savings & Loan that was now his. Seth Spencer, said the brass nameplate on his office door. President.

Not that Jenna would care. Against his will, Seth visualized her Soho loft, the tasseled pillows, stacked books, and rock-hard, thigh-high queen-size bed that was perfect for lovemaking. The image was razor-sharp since Seth had showered, shaved and slept there with enough regularity over the past year and a half that the place felt like home.

Jenna had been naked in bed when he told her he was leaving a job at Goldman Sachs to return to Tyler as president of the family's S&L, since his father, Elias, was retiring.

"Wonderful," was all Jenna had said.

"Wonderful," he muttered now. She hadn't voiced concern for the future of their relationship, nor asked if he wanted to keep in touch. In fact, she hadn't even quit painting her toenails. Even now he could see her: wearing a crimson nightie, sitting on the mussed covers of the bed, tilting a bottle of mint-green polish in one hand and brushing the nail of her baby toe with the other. She hadn't been the least perturbed that he was leaving. Why couldn't he just accept it?

He blew out another sigh, this one more murderous than the last. And why was that ugly gold junker still idling? Was it really Jenna? Was she waiting for him to notice her? To come out and strike up a conversation?

"If that's what you're thinking, sweetheart, keep dreaming," Seth whispered around the unlit cigar, unaware his posture was exactly as it had been twenty-three years ago, on Thanksgiving Day, when he'd sat ponderously at his father's kitchen table after hearing that his mother had disappeared. Later that day, he'd been told she'd run off with Ray Bennedict. Before nightfall, Seth had decided his mother was never coming back, and he'd promised himself he wouldn't hope for a phone call or a knock at the door. He wouldn't torture himself with the usual, ridiculous adolescent fantasies…wouldn't imagine his mother coming to the schoolyard fence, her haunted eyes searching for him and his brothers, Quinn and Brady....

No, once she left, it was best never to expect a woman to return.

Seth leaned forward, anyway, wishing the woman in the Cadillac didn't look so much like Jenna. He didn't trust his perceptions, though, no more than he could admit how her lovemaking had affected him. Model-tall and fire-hot, Jenna had burned in his arms like a flaming torch. She possessed wild, short, red-streaked hair and a trendy wardrobe of sequined sweaters, feathered earrings and capes that electrified Seth's every last male nerve. Where he strictly wore muted browns and grays, Jenna's wardrobe exploded in magenta and turquoise, violet and crimson. All brightly colored motion, she'd been like a bird, flitting around him while Seth stayed still as a statue.

Somehow they'd fit, though.

"Our bodies sure did," he growled, gritting his teeth against the sudden, unwanted ache of his groin. Ever since he'd happened into the Soho gallery where she worked, he and Jenna had dated. Not seriously, they'd assured each other, even though they'd wound up in bed on the first date. The next evening, on the second, they'd ordered takeout and made love while devouring Chinese food, and on the third date they'd quit bothering with the food.

But it was only sex, they'd said. Unusual chemical attraction. Nothing more.

They'd even gone months between dates as if to prove their continued emotional sovereignty. But now, as Seth stared at the car idling in the road, he admitted the truth. He still wanted her. He missed her like the devil.

Maybe *he* should have initiated a talk about their relationship before he left New York, but Jenna knew that wasn't his style, didn't she? Sighing, he tried to ignore the panic in his gut. He shouldn't have minded the feeling. He was used to money deals and playing daily roulette with the stock market, and now that he had his own bank, the stakes were even higher. But when he made banking decisions, rows of neat, orderly figures backed him up. The panic he felt now was different. This panic was female-related, and Seth knew next to nothing about females.

Banking, he understood. Slowly and steadily, he'd worked for years, garnering the experience needed to run the S&L, a business in which his brothers Quinn and Brady had no personal interest. Seth had followed their father's every step, going from Columbia to Wharton, then to Goldman Sachs—all so that now, at the age of thirty-seven, he could run this bank.

He'd never imagined that only six weeks after taking the job he'd be fighting the urge to turn his back on everything he'd ever worked for, just so he could return to New York and Jenna. *Jenna, who doesn't even want you.*

The Cadillac started moving again.

His heart missed a beat.

But no, it really couldn't be Jenna. She was from a Podunk North Carolina town she'd professed to hate, and once she'd left for the big city, she'd never

looked back. Jenna would never venture into a place
that lacked a cappuccino bar, a foreign film theater or
inch-thick tabloids dripping with juicy celebrity gossip. Not that Tyler lacked gossip, Seth thought with
remembered anger, his broad, powerful back stiffen-
ing to ward off buried emotions left over from ado-
lescence. After his mother ran off with Ray, Seth had
endured more than his share of pitying glances and
hushed whispers. It hurt having the whole town know
the Spencers hadn't been man enough to hang on to
the woman they loved.

It was why, if Seth was honest, he'd rather be any-
where in the world than Tyler, Wisconsin, this time
of year. October was nearly gone, and Canadian air—
cold, crisp and thin—was sweeping south into the re-
gion and chilling him to the bone.

Twenty years, he thought. Hard to believe, but it
had been twenty years since he'd lived in Tyler. A
lifetime. He'd been sure that when he came back
home, the old feelings of loss and longing would be
gone, but this was cold, hard, wintry country, with
glassy lakes and too much empty space, the kind of
country that always left a man with too much time
on his hands to think about his past.

One too many nights Seth had needed Jenna to
keep him warm. Now he cursed the stranger in the
car for making him remember how her soft, smooth
skin had burned under his greedy hands, and how
easily her damp, wanting mouth had slackened for
his, memories that made his groin tighten.

Memories, Seth thought, were damn powerful things.

Outside, the car swerved. Silently, he watched the headlights sweeping the pavement as the car rounded a corner, then disappeared. Only then did he rise. He kept staring into the dark, his eyes inadvertently searching, his heart aching with familiar loss and the firmly held conviction that once a woman was gone from a man's life, she never returned.

"WHERE'S THE Kelsey Boarding House?" Jenna Robinson groaned, twisting the sparkling engagement ring on her finger and glancing into the rearview mirror, to where Gretchen was strapped in a car seat. "Hey there, sweetie," she added. "You holding up okay?"

The two-year-old yawned.

Jenna chuckled. Gretchen looked adorable, dressed in black corduroy overalls and a pint-size black leather jacket. "We're almost there," Jenna assured, freeing a hand and flattening Molly Blake's directions against the cracked vinyl of the ample dashboard. Staring through the windshield, Jenna tried to ignore her hammering heart. "What was I thinking?" she murmured, knowing she shouldn't have stopped outside the S&L. Was Seth working? Or had he left the office for the day?

"Jenna, you're pathetic." She had only one piece of business to take care of in Tyler, Wisconsin—informing Seth she was getting married next week. And who could blame her for wanting to deliver the news as soon as possible? After she'd endured a painful year and a half of Seth's noncommittal behavior, somebody else had fallen desperately in love with her and wanted to help her raise the baby she was carrying. Just thinking of the life growing inside her made her eyes soften.

Seth's baby.

Pushing aside the thought, she decided that she had to get some rest and change clothes before she told him the news. She was covered with road grime. Besides, one look around the Madison airport had made perfectly clear that Jenna was all wrong for Wisconsin, not that her fishnet stockings, feathered sweater and miniskirt were *that* strange. Nor did she think she'd packed anything much more conservative. Nevertheless, she was tired of people staring at her as if she were wearing a Halloween costume. "This place could sure use some action," she muttered, glancing around the dark, tree-lined street. With Halloween upcoming, maybe she'd dress as a bank robber and target the Spencer family's bank.

Meantime, every horse, wire fence and mile on the odometer of the Cadillac reminded her of why she'd fled Bear Creek, North Carolina, for the Fashion Institute of New York the second she turned eighteen. Her hands tightened on the wheel as she thought of North Carolina and her parents, not that she exactly wanted to dwell on Nancy and Ralph, who were so close they'd scarcely ever seemed to notice their daughter existed. It was probably why Jenna had so foolishly pursued Seth, willing to take the crumbs he called affection.

"Face it, Jenna, it's your cross to bear." She glanced at the faded paperback cover of *Women Who Love Too Much,* which was beside her on the seat. She'd brought it to reread on the plane. When it came to attracting unavailable men, she was like the magnet inside an MRI.

Or she *had* been.

But now she was loved. Cherished. Cared for in the exact way she deserved. Her throat tightening, she thought of the Soho art gallery owned by her friend, Sue Ellis, who was Gretchen's mom, and then she thought of the gallery's co-owner, Dom Milano.

Even now, she could barely believe Dom had proposed. Buoyed up by the passion he'd expressed, Jenna felt her heart ache. She'd met the two gallery owners only a week after moving to New York, and over the past sixteen years, they'd become her substitute family. It was why Jenna had agreed, at the eleventh hour, to watch Gretchen while Sue went on an impromptu art buying trip to Paris.

Fortunately, Gretchen had handled the airplane like a pro. Jenna had felt antsy about bringing the baby to Tyler, but Dom had his hands full with running the gallery right now, and he insisted Jenna talk to Seth before she responded to the marriage proposal.

Jenna simply couldn't wait. She was going to marry Dom as soon as she returned to New York. He was such a sweetheart. He'd said he wouldn't start their physical relationship—not so much as a kiss, he'd vowed—until she went to Tyler, until he knew she would definitely be his. She smiled weakly. Who would have known Dom could be so romantic? In all the years of their friendship, she never would have guessed.

And he was so sexy. Tall and slender, he was Italian-born and raised on Mott Street in Little Italy. He had straight black hair, devastating dark eyes, and after sixteen years of knowing him, Jenna knew she'd never find a better man. He was so accommodating, too, guessing Jenna's needs before she even knew she had them. What she'd shared with Seth, she assured herself, was nothing more than overrated chemistry.

She frowned. Since Sue's divorce, Jenna had felt so sure Dom was falling for Sue, though. He'd doted on Gretchen, too. Mistakenly, Jenna had assumed that the time Dom spent with Jenna wasn't significant, especially since they usually went over strategies for strengthening her relationship with Seth. After Seth left for Tyler, Dom had overheard her speaking on the phone with an obstetrician, and he'd proposed.

He'd been so eloquent, too. He said he wanted her, loved her. He offered her everything she secretly wanted—marriage and a name for the baby. But Dom had one condition: that she come to Tyler and tell Seth about the pregnancy, just to ensure there wouldn't be trouble later. Which, of course, there wouldn't be. Seth couldn't care less.

Blowing out a shaky breath, she murmured, "How did I manage to get lost in a town this small? Where's the boarding house?" Her eyes traced the street, the frame houses reminding her that she wasn't going to a four-star hotel. No *USA Today* and room service. "Ah," she suddenly said, "that must be it. The address is right."

Fortunately, there was plenty of room to park. Jenna hadn't driven for years. She'd never been behind the wheel of a car this large, either, but it had been the least expensive at the rent-a-wreck. Getting out, she slammed the door, then lifted Gretchen from the back seat, deciding to check in before retrieving their suitcases from the car. "Hey, sweetie," she murmured again, planting a kiss on Gretchen's cheek and grinning down as the toddler's short stubby legs wrapped around her waist.

Gretchen blinked, curling sleepily on Jenna's shoulder as they headed for the door. Frowning, Jenna suddenly wished she hadn't agreed to do work for Molly Blake. "You're so spineless," she whispered aloud, her breath fogging the chilly air. A month or so ago, Seth had given her Molly's number, saying Molly was thinking of opening a bed-and-breakfast and might want to hire a freelance artist to do some promotion. Seth, of course, assumed Jenna would do the work via mail from New York.

And she should have. That way she could talk to Seth, just as she'd promised Dom, then leave immediately. Still, without having a reason other than her and Seth Spencer's baby, she simply couldn't bring herself to come to Tyler.

Anxiously twisting the ring on her finger again, she winced, hoping Sue and Dom found the note in the gallery saying she'd borrowed it. Dom said they'd shop for a ring as soon as she returned; meantime, she'd decided to give Seth the message loud and clear that she was getting married. Seth didn't have to know this was a cubic zircon, not a real diamond.

"Hello," she called, shifting Gretchen as she unzipped her black leather coat, opened the door of the boarding house and stepped inside, relieved to find the place clean and bright, bustling with early evening activity. "You must be Johnny Kelsey."

"Sure am." The man was in his sixties, had dark hair shot through with gray, and Jenna was relieved to see he was the first resident of Wisconsin who didn't seem the least perturbed by fishnets and leather. "That must be Gretchen," he continued. "We got a crib set up for her. Over there, that's Patrick and Pam," he said, nodding toward his son and his son's wife.

Jenna nodded. "Ah," she returned, smiling. "Molly mentioned you." Molly had also said Pam Kelsey was an Olympic track medallist before being diagnosed with MS. Apparently, her health was good now, and the couple had adopted a son, Jeremy, now four. Before Jenna could continue, Johnny said, "And this fine young lady is Caroline Benning. She's working at our best eatery in town, Marge's Diner, so I'm sure you'll meet again. Her room's just down the hallway from yours."

"Hi," Jenna said, her eyes settling on the other woman. She was young, in her early twenties and all-American-pretty, tall and willowy with bright green eyes and light brown, highlighted hair. She'd been coming from the back of the house, carrying a quilt which she'd probably shaken out. When Gretchen leaned in, reaching for the bright fabric, Caroline stepped back, almost protectively.

"Now, don't get so grabby, Gretchen," Jenna said with a soft laugh, curling her hand gently over Gretchen's chubby fingers and distracting her. "Lovely quilt work," she added, her eyes taking in the handiwork. Before she could further study the design, Johnny Kelsey captured her attention again. "No baggage, Ms. Robinson?"

Baggage? She had plenty, of course, but Johnny wasn't really inquiring about her relationship with Seth Spencer. She laughed again. "Do I look like a woman who travels without suitcases?"

He looked her over as if contemplating everything from her blue fingernail polish, to the decorative collar stenciled around her neck in henna, to her studded earlobes and clothes, then he chuckled. "Somehow I bet you've got more than one."

"Please call me Jenna," she corrected with a smile. "The things are in the car." Pausing, she grinned down at Gretchen who was asleep on her shoulder. "I figure I'd better put this sleepy little rascal down first, though."

And then Jenna would tell Seth Spencer she was pregnant.

Chapter Two

"Jenna couldn't have stirred up Tyler, Wisconsin any more than this if she morphed into an Osterizer blender," Seth murmured the next morning, staring through the open door of his private office toward the windows in the lobby. Deciding against shrugging into the muted brown suit jacket that matched his slacks, he ignored the hammering of his heart as she parallel parked in front of the bank. Or, more accurately, *tried* to parallel park.

Nervously, he knotted an olive tie that was neatly tucked under the collar of a white shirt he'd pressed himself. Six weeks hadn't been enough time to adjust to not having Chinese laundries where he could drop off his shirts, but watching Jenna, he suddenly wished he'd done a better job of ironing his rumpled sleeves and cuffs. He looked the last way he wanted to—like a man desperately in need of a woman's care.

Despite his apprehension—or, more accurately, *hope* about what Jenna was doing in Tyler—Seth smiled, taking in her seventh attempt to wedge the noisy, dented gold tank between Nora Gates Forres-

ter's new Miata roadster and Marge Phelps's red
Dodge truck. Jenna, who hadn't yet realized she had
a good six feet to spare, was now drawing a crowd
on the sidewalk. ''If more people show up, maybe I'll
sell popcorn and peanuts,'' mused Seth. ''Maybe
even funnel cakes.''

Not that Jenna looked particularly pleased about
having an audience. Knowing her, the Smashing
Pumpkins or Nirvana were blasting from the radio,
anyway, so she wouldn't hear anybody coaching. Because of the way she was hunched over the wheel,
turning it with all her might, Seth figured the Cadillac
lacked power steering. As she painstakingly angled
between the other two cars, she craned her head toward the child who was strapped in back, then
whirled toward the windshield again.

Even from here, she looked so gorgeous that Seth's
breath caught. His heart clutched, too, not that his
impenetrable features would allow anyone to guess it.
He knew right then that Jenna Robinson wasn't leaving his office until they made love on the smooth,
polished mahogany surface of his desk. If the truth
be told, he'd been fantasizing about that for weeks.
A plan formed as he swept the work papers into a
drawer. The second she came through the door, he'd
kiss her senseless, pull her against his chest and hold
her as if he'd never let go. Gently, he'd lift her, carry
her to the desk and...

The more he thought about the countless things he
wanted to do and say to her, the more Seth admitted

he'd never wanted a woman so badly. "Unbelievable," he whispered.

Jenna Robinson was really in Tyler, Wisconsin. Maybe she cared about him, after all. When he got to work this morning, he'd heard the news about her arrival, but he hadn't really believed it. After the way his mother had left Tyler years ago, maybe he'd never fully believe a woman could care for him. Old emotions died hard, he guessed. The well-oiled Tyler gossip machine turned out to be right, though. After all, it wasn't every day that a gold Cadillac lurched into Tyler.

This was the story Seth had gotten: Feeling naturally curious, Nora Gates Forrester had called Martha Bauer at Worthington House last night in hopes of finding out who the woman in the gold Cadillac was, since Martha usually knew everything. Martha couldn't identify Jenna, however, so the two women conference-called Tisha, who was still at The Hair Affair. No one having their hair done had recognized Jenna, but after she checked into the boarding house, Anna Kelsey kindly called Lydia Perry, who then called Reverend Sarah Baron, who called Jenna at Kelsey's to say her husband, Michael, wanted to look at the car muffler and to invite Jenna to Sunday services at the Tyler Fellowship Sanctuary—all of which meant that by the time Molly Blake arrived at the S&L this morning to discuss the loan for the bed-and-breakfast she wanted to open, he'd already found out from his brother that the new resident at Kelsey's was Jenna.

"Jenna Robinson?" Seth had asked Molly anyway. As much as he hated gossip, he had been unable to stop himself from asking for more confirmation. "You're sure, Molly?"

Molly had frowned as if suddenly terrified her loan might be jeopardized by her association with Jenna. "I hope that's all right," she'd said worriedly. "You did recommend her, didn't you? I'm getting together with Jenna today, to discuss the promotional materials for the bed-and-breakfast…materials I'd hoped she could share with you tomorrow. I thought you two were friends…"

"We dated in New York," Seth assured her.

Before he could remind Molly that he was a banker, not an ogre, Molly raced on, "Oh, good! Jenna sounded so nice on the phone, and she begged me to keep this news of her coming to Tyler a secret, so I did. I guess my saying so now doesn't matter, since you know she's here, but she wanted her arrival to be a surprise. She must simply adore you." Molly lowered her voice. "And we all saw the cute little girl with her. She was strapped in the—"

"Back seat?" Seth had said, grinning but raising his eyes in surprise. "She's about two? Chubby, with a big grin and squinched up nose? A spray of blond hair she keeps pulled back in bow-shaped barrettes?"

Molly giggled. "Sounds about right."

"That's Jenna's boss's daughter," Seth hadn't been able to stop himself from confiding, feeling eager for news of Jenna. Sure, he dreaded getting more deeply involved and courting the old, hurtful feelings left by his mother's abandonment, but nothing more than hearing Jenna's name practically did him in. It felt good in his mouth; speaking it reminded him of the dark, sensual hours they'd spent, and even now, he could almost feel her hair catching on his lips. "Jenna's like a second mother to Gretchen," he'd added with a frown, thinking of the child he'd come to know while dating Jenna. "It seems strange that she brought Gretchen here, though."

"Oh," Molly had laughed, blushing. "And here I was thinking the baby was— Oh, I don't know what I was thinking, Mr. Spencer! I just guessed that maybe…"

Seth couldn't help but catch Molly's drift. "That the baby was mine?" A soft, startled chuckle had escaped his lips. The idea had taken him by surprise, but shouldn't he have considered fatherhood before now? He was thirty-seven. Some men his age had kids who were heading off for college. If the truth be told, Seth liked the idea of kids; they were cute, funny and sweet. It was only women that worried him. "No wonder you want to open the Breakfast Inn Bed," he'd managed to say aloud to Molly. "You're obviously a romantic."

"True, but the inn will be profitable," Molly assured, her eyes narrowing as she continued surveying Seth. "Maybe I shouldn't tell you this, but you're right. I'm a romantic. Since you said you and Jenna dated in New York, maybe you should know that everybody took note of the wedding dress in the front seat of her car. Everybody wants to know if you two are…''

Somehow, he'd controlled his shocked expression, his mind reeling. Jenna had brought a wedding dress to Tyler? ''Considering getting married?'' he'd finished for Molly. ''Not that I know of. If Jenna's got that on her mind, she sure hasn't informed me yet.''

Now he swallowed hard, his throat feeling dry and raw. What could be the meaning of Jenna's bringing a wedding dress to Tyler? He was definitely the only man she knew here. Had he been wrong for the past six weeks? Had she really missed him as much as he'd secretly missed her? Had he been a fool not to offer her more trust?

''Looks like she might have come here to propose to me,'' he murmured, feeling stupefied as he blew out a shaky breath.

Earlier, he'd been so overwhelmed that he'd barely heard the rest of Molly's spiel as they'd continued discussing the status of her loan. Unfortunately, in addition to needing start-up capital, a neighbor who didn't relish having a business next door to her was causing Molly some trouble. Seth hoped things would work out. He liked Molly immensely and wanted to give her the money, but protocol demanded he see her property first, something he'd said he'd do tomorrow with Jenna, since Molly wanted him to review Jenna's plans for creating promotional materials.

By tomorrow I'll be engaged. The voice came from nowhere, and Seth realized it was probably true, given that Jenna had breezed into Tyler with the wedding dress. "A wedding dress?" he'd said at one point to Molly. "Are you absolutely positive? You really saw this?"

Molly had nodded. "You could see it plain as day in the front seat of that car," she'd assured. "I wasn't that close, but Nora was in the window of her department store working on the Halloween display, so she got a better look. The streetlight was shining right into the car, she said, so she could see that the dress was of lace and sequins, and since it took up half the front seat, Nora figures it's floor-length with a full skirt. If a veil's needed, Nora said she just got some in for the bridal boutique. You know," Molly added, "the one she just opened in her store."

Seth hadn't heard about the boutique, but there was enough detail in the description to convince him the rumor about the wedding dress was true. Strangely, none of his usual panic had descended when he thought of standing at the altar with Jenna. Deep down, he trusted her, didn't he? He'd known her a long time. Hell, some couples tied the knot after knowing each other only a few weeks, right? And it sure did look as if Jenna had come all the way out to the boondocks to claim him.

Sure, he'd felt a little worried last night when he'd only *thought* the woman in the car was Jenna. But now he *knew* it was her. And if she'd come all the way to Tyler with a wedding dress, couldn't he assume she'd want to make some kind of commitment? Didn't that mean she might not abandon him in the future? All this time he'd told himself he was marriage-shy, but wasn't that merely defensiveness?

Now he watched her get regally out of the car, her tall, slim body floating upward. She slammed the door and leaned into the back seat for Gretchen. A smile tugged his lips when he saw the baby girl he'd come to adore. A black knit cap was snuggled down around her ears, and Jenna had dressed her in black jeans and a leather jacket. Unbidden came the thought, *Why not have kids of our own? I'm thirty-seven, and Jenna's only thirty-four, so it's not too late. There's plenty of time.* He thought of how much he'd loved hanging around with his brothers, Quinn and Brady, when they were kids, and of how much fun he'd had when he, Sue, Dom and Jenna had taken Gretchen trick-or-treating for the first time last Halloween. That was exactly a year ago. Suddenly, it seemed hard not to imagine Jenna—craftsy as she was—making costumes for their kids. In a year or two, maybe he and Jenna really would have a child....

"I don't know," he murmured. Maybe he was jumping the gun. Maybe Molly had gotten things all wrong, and there was no wedding dress. Seth guessed he'd find out the truth soon enough.

Outside, Jenna stepped around the Cadillac and to the curb, and he drew in yet another sharp breath at the sight of her. Six weeks without her had definitely been rough. In fact, right now he felt as if someone had given him a shot of straight testosterone. Despite that, he chuckled and shook his head, seeing that

Brick Bauer and Lee Nielsen had stopped on the sidewalk to gape at her.

Any man would.

Yes, indeed, Jenna Robinson was quite a sight for Tyler. As usual, she'd done something new, inventive and wild with her hair. Jagged streaks of red shot through the jaw-length, auburn strands, and the cut made it look as if she were wearing a cap of soft, exotic feathers. Involuntarily, Seth's fingers flexed with the need to touch it, then he licked where his lips had gone dry. Around the long, slender column of her swanlike neck someone—probably Gretchen's mom, Sue—had painted a temporary henna design that resembled a lace choker.

Everything inside him tightened as his eyes drifted down to where the sides of a chic, A-lined, thigh-high black leather coat fell open over a tight, powder blue lace top, and by the time Seth's eyes hit her miniskirt, he was a complete goner. A groan escaped him as he took in the hip-hugging fabric. "What am I going to do with you, lady?" he whispered.

She had the sort of endless, mouth-watering legs that went on for miles, and that seemed to beg a man to bend them and kiss the tender taut flesh behind her knees. Right now those scrumptious legs were encased in silver, black-patterned tights. Tall, skinny, knee-high boots were threaded with red laces that zigzagged up her slender calves.

By some miracle she didn't look the least bit trampy. Given her clothes, she should have. But Jenna could slip into the most outrageous attire and waltz down a sidewalk looking like a centerfold for *Class* magazine. Her features were simply too refined to allow for the wrong impression. Her heart-shaped face was delicate and finely boned, and she held her perfectly formed mouth almost primly as if to ensure onlookers that she didn't put up with any nonsense. The expression wasn't just for show, either, as Seth well knew. On occasion, Jenna Robinson was a girl who came out—loud and proud—as a girl with attitude.

Her strange mix of prim censure and vampiness had first captured Seth's attention—and imagination—nearly two years ago. Now his gaze riveted on her eyes, or at least what he could see of them, since they were obscured by round, wire-rimmed sunglasses.

Shifting Gretchen on her hip, she resolutely headed toward the front doors of the bank, making Seth feel more oddly nervous than he had in his whole life. All at once, he was aware that his palms had gotten damp, something that hadn't even happened during the last stock market crash. Today was different, though. Infinitely more nerve-racking. Not only had the woman he'd left back in New York shown up in Tyler, but she'd apparently come bearing a wedding dress.

"Here's to you, Ms. Robinson," he whispered.

"How could you let this happen?" Jenna mouthed worriedly. Once Seth met her in the bank's lobby and said hello in that smooth, melodious baritone that drove her so wild, she should have known her plans would derail. They always did.

Just looking at him had filled her with hopelessness. How could she tell him she was marrying Dom? Sure, she'd lain awake all night, carefully imagining herself charging into Tyler's S&L to deliver her rehearsed speech about being pregnant and getting married. She'd practiced until she felt fully prepared for the encounter, buoyed up by Dom's proposal and the fact that she was six weeks pregnant with a baby who needed a father. *Dom loves you, Dom loves you, Dom loves you,* she'd reminded herself, the words going through her mind like a mantra this morning as she'd gripped the wheel and rounded the town square in Tyler, driving toward the bank.

"All this time we've worked together," she'd remembered Dom saying, his gentle voice brimming with emotion, "my feelings for you have grown, Jenna. And now that Seth's back in Tyler, it's my first real chance to tell you how deeply I feel, to ask you to marry me."

"Somebody loves me," she'd whispered when the S&L came into sight. "No matter what Seth says, I won't forget Dom's waiting for me in New York." Countless times this morning, she'd changed clothes, and at least until she'd arrived on Main Street, U.S.A., she'd been sure her outfit was conservative enough for the bank...conservative enough to show Seth she was calm, cool, collected and not the least bit ruffled by how easily he'd left New York and their relationship.

When she'd gotten out of the car in Tyler, however, people had turned to stare, immediately reminding her of why she'd fled Bear Creek, North Carolina, years ago.

Well, let people look, she'd fumed silently as she'd headed inside the bank with Gretchen, working herself into a tizzy, already imagining her final, grand exit. She'd tell Seth, once and for all, that she didn't need him, that everything was different now. Dom loved her so much he'd proposed, she'd announce boldly, then she'd push through the lobby doors and head straight back to New York. Imagination being what it was, she kept seeing herself hop into something far flashier than the dented Cadillac.

Not that it mattered. Like all best-laid plans, something had gone terribly wrong, and before Jenna could even open her mouth, Seth had chuckled. ''Some car you've got there. I hope it was free.''

Was that all he intended to say after six weeks of separation? After Jenna had traveled all the way across the country to see him? She'd glared at him. ''Are you saying you have a problem with my car?''

''Nope. It's better entertainment than a movie. Everybody in Tyler's talking about it. Martha Bauer swears it once belonged to Elvis, and when Jack Moray came in to deposit his weekly checks, he admitted he almost towed it from where it was parked in front of the Kelsey Boarding House last night.''

Curious in spite of herself, she'd said, ''Jack Moray?''

Seth had nodded. "He's a tow-truck owner. He thought it was abandoned, but Michael stopped him."

"Michael?"

"The minister's husband."

"Oh, right. Sarah Baron. She's the minister who called me," Jenna had said, hating to admit how much she'd warmed to the show of down-home hospitality. She truly did despise small towns, she'd assured herself, and since Seth Spencer now lived in one, Jenna was very determined to keep it that way.

"And the man at the curb," he'd continued, "the one staring at your inspection sticker. That's Cooper Night Hawk. He's a deputy."

"I'm legal."

Leveling her with an assessing male stare that had her fighting a shiver, Seth had softly returned, "You sure as hell don't *look* legal, Jenna."

"Come near me and you'll get arrested."

"You brought handcuffs?"

She'd shot Seth a look of censure. "Manacles."

"Hope you'll want to throw away the keys."

At that tantalizing juncture, she'd at least gotten out the first five words of her planned speech. "Seth, we need to talk."

"We'll start with sweet nothings and go from there," he'd assured lightly, the words of promise turning her legs to water.

By the time Jenna found herself standing in his office, she'd decided it was hopeless. Even moments before, as she'd steeled herself against him, Seth had managed to relieve her of Gretchen so quickly that the baby could have been a greased watermelon. He'd placed a guiding hand under Jenna's elbow in that damnably sexy, gentlemanly gesture she was so determined to forget, the one that made her feel so much like a woman, and the next thing she'd known, he'd been slipping her coat from her shoulders and employing a bank teller to baby-sit Gretchen.

Now Jenna stared around his office. "Well," she managed dryly, "here we are."

Smiling, Seth shut the door, then quickly twisted the lock.

Her mouth dropped. She'd missed him physically, but she definitely had more self-respect than this. Holding out her hands, palms up, she schooled herself not to lose her nerve. "What I have to say isn't *that* private." She glared pointedly at the lock.

"No?"

Seth didn't look convinced. In fact, he looked completely, unnervingly in control, reminding Jenna of exactly why she'd come. For once, it would be a pleasure to tell this man she had her own agenda. Her heart missed a beat. Why did the father of her coming baby have to be so handsome and commanding? Ever since she'd first laid eyes on Seth Spencer, she'd found him irresistible. He was a good six inches taller than she—six-foot-two to her five-eight—with dark brown, chocolate-colored hair he kept neatly trimmed over his ears. Slightly spiked bangs jagged onto a high forehead, accentuating brown eyes that shouldn't have been so interesting, but that did crazy things to her insides, anyway. His squarish face was set with a

hard, practical mouth that reminded her of how well
he kissed and hinted at the mysterious moody silences
she'd come to expect from him on occasion. Why was
he so moody, though, she wondered now. What com-
plaints could Seth have? He'd told her his mother had
died years ago, but otherwise, his seemed to be a
trauma-free childhood in a town that Norman Rock-
well could have painted. As far as Jenna knew, he'd
always been successful in his undertakings, not to
mention groomed from birth to run this bank.

Whatever the case, Seth's looks shouldn't have
made him so mouth-watering, but he was, and that
annoyed her. Well, that, and the rumpled shirt he'd
tucked into soft brown wool trousers that looked far
too expensive for Tyler. The damn shirt made Jenna
want to do the most foolhardy things for him, like set
up an ironing board in his living room. Even worse,
the bemused tilt of that hard, uncompromising mouth
said Seth knew it.

"I'm waiting," he said.

"Unlock that door."

His lips stretched further, in a smile that both
warmed and irritated. "Why? So you can run for the
lobby, Jen?"

Jen. Why did he have to call me Jen? Jen was a
pet name he reserved for special moments, such as
when they were naked and wrapped in each other's
arms. She braced herself. Mentally rehearsing her
speech for the last time, she felt unreality sweep
through her. Suddenly, she felt like a bit player in a
bad, low-budget zombie film, as if she was locked

inside a room with Seth Spencer, but she couldn't move or speak. It was as if an unseen hand had just appeared from nowhere and clamped down hard over her mouth. *I'm pregnant and marrying Dom. Just say it!*

Seth was still smiling.

And despite the promises to herself, something in Jenna's heart gave. She didn't want to react to him, no more than she wanted to react to this bank. The Tyler Savings & Loan, she thought. Seth's bank. It was just as he'd so often described it to her, a simple brick building with a clock tower overlooking the town square. He'd always sounded so proud.

Maybe I'm being too hard on him, she found herself thinking as she gazed into brown eyes that were so ordinary and yet so strangely beguiling. She'd always known he was going to return to Tyler someday, right? It wasn't as if the man had lied. Maybe it wasn't right to drop the news on her so casually, but he'd never made a secret of the fact that he was being groomed for this job. Still…

I thought he'd gotten serious about me and would ask me to come.

But he hadn't. And years of living with Ralph and Nancy Robinson had made Jenna tired of settling for less love than she deserved. Pushing aside the thoughts, she tried to hold onto her resolve. She was definitely marrying Dom within the week. It was the right thing to do, both for herself and the coming baby. It hurt, but she forced herself to think about how much time she and Seth had spent apart. Even while they'd dated, he'd made clear that he didn't want to deepen the relationship. He'd never warmed to the topic of having a family…

Despite the circumstances, she found herself craving just one kiss from him. "You look good, Seth." The words slipped out.

"You don't look bad yourself, Jen."

She edged back, against the door, her eyes darting around the simple, well-appointed office. She frowned when she saw the clear top of his polished wooden desk, and she wondered if he was happy with his move. "Doesn't look like you're keeping yourself too busy around here," she said with concern. He'd always been so active on Wall Street.

"That," Seth murmured, angling his body toward hers, "or I've got plans for the desk."

Those damnably irresistible lights in his eyes made clear what he meant. "Plans?"

Leaning swiftly, he grasped her fingers, the touch of his skin sending a current of electricity dancing up her arm. Panicking, her knees weakening, she told herself to let go of Seth's hand, but something in its smooth heat made her twine her fingers through his. Stepping backward, he pulled her toward the desk, and even though her heart was beating out of control, she followed. *Tell him about the baby! Tell him you're marrying Dom!* screamed a voice in her mind.

Another said, *If you don't make love with him now, Jenna, you'll never get another chance. It's only sex to Seth, nothing more, but you'll always miss the feel of his arms wrapped around you. If you don't do this now, you'll never feel his chest, hard and crushing against yours, again, or the pounding of his heart. You'll never have the opportunity to feel so physically close to a man again. What you share with him is so special, not something you'll find with Dom.*

Her hind end hit the desk. As Seth lowered her to the surface, she gasped. Scents of expensive aftershave and cologne came in tandem with starch from his shirt as his strong, warm body covered hers. Their hips locked. Just as she registered his arousal, he angled his head downward, his lips hovering. She opened her mouth, knowing things had gone too far. She had to tell him about Dom. Now! "Seth—"

His mouth covered hers. The swift capture of her lips communicated full intent, and the onslaught of his tongue challenged, plunging deeply, wetly. Long ago they'd discussed safe sex and knew they were both healthy, but on occasions such as this, they'd sometimes made love without protection like teenage fools. It was how she'd gotten pregnant. And since she already was, she figured there was no danger now. *Except that you're getting married!* said a voice. But then, she hadn't really said yes yet, had she?

"Seth," she suddenly protested.

"Jen," he'd murmured simply. "Oh, Jen."

She tried to find her voice again, but she'd missed him too much over the past six weeks, and the power of his kisses were more than she could stand. Later, she'd be furious over her lack of willpower. Later, she'd be worried about this momentary, understandable lapse, but she'd tell herself she had every right to go through with her plans to marry another man.

Besides, Seth didn't care, did he?

Her mind hazed as her hands cupped his shoulders, then glided over the back of his crisp cotton shirt. No, Seth didn't care, she told herself as a dark strong hand slid effortlessly down her lace top, opening the buttons, right before effortlessly opening the front catch of her bra. No, he could never love her, she gasped as his mouth covered a nipple, the slow, sensual swirls of his tongue seeming to touch the core of her.

She wanted to feel his chest.

That was her last coherent thought as her hands fumbled with the knot of his tie, then the buttons of his shirt. Pushing apart the sides, her palms cupped rock-hard pectorals, then her fingers delved hungrily into hairs that felt like tangled silk. Vaguely, she was thinking about the fact that he probably didn't want children. No, whenever she'd commented on how cute they were, playing in the parks in New York, he'd never said anything affirming.

Now his hands glided up her outer thighs, pushing up the skirt she should have known better than to wear because she knew how much it would arouse him. She tried not to buy into the illusion she'd allowed herself for the past year and a half, the illusion that Seth really did care, but only spoke through his body, rather than in words. It was a nice illusion. And it seemed so plausible right now. Surely, no man kissed like this if he didn't love a woman.

"Seth," his name escaped with a soft moan, the

core of her aching as he drew down her tights and panties.

"Jen," he whispered again, his blistering hot mouth sweeping hers again as his trousers dropped. And then he was inside her. Feeling him so deeply filling her, she flung back her head, drifting to a place where only he could take her. No man had ever given her this kind of pleasure. Suddenly, she wanted to cry, knowing she could never live without this kind of passion, but that she'd have to. *I should have...should told him,* she thought incoherently. *Have to tell him right now...* And then the thoughts were gone and she shattered. His release came with hers, tearing at her heart. Wasn't this kind of perfectly choreographed sex almost unheard of?

But Seth didn't love her! She had to move on, to marry Dom. Her senses still reeling, she quickly began to right her clothes, furious at herself but knowing she had a responsibility to herself and to the coming baby. Forget Seth! She was starting a family.

"Seth," she managed weakly, her body still awash with his heat as she slid off the desk, tugging down her skirt. "I can't believe this happened," she began, running a hand through her hair. "But I know you'll understand. I think we can talk reasonably. We've known each other such a long time, shared so much, and while I know we've never...uh, pretended to mean more to each other, I think we can speak openly here."

Nodding, he buckled his belt, shooting her a gentle smile. "All of Tyler's wondering why you're in town.

And so am I. So, go ahead and say whatever's on your mind.''

''I know it's only been six weeks,'' she began, wishing she hadn't made love to him, but trying to tell herself this visit was still going fine, that she could recoup her losses, ''however, a lot's happened since you left New York.''

Looking pleased in a way she couldn't quite understand, Seth eyed her playfully as he knotted his tie. ''Go on.''

Forcing herself not to notice that those irresistible dark brown eyes were as warm as whiskey mixed with liquid smoke, she tried to prioritize her thoughts, then she forced herself to continue. ''I…well, the first thing I guess you should know is that Dom and I are getting married.''

Chapter Three

"Married? After what we just did?" Seth managed, unable to process what she'd just said. Surely he'd misunderstood. Jenna wasn't marrying another man! She couldn't! His body was still on fire. His thighs were weak from how she'd sapped every last drop of his strength, and his voice was low and raspy from the raw way he'd kept whispering her name. "You're telling me this after making love to me, Jenna?"

"We didn't make love," she protested nervously, quickly buttoning her top and tucking it into her leather miniskirt. "We had sex." She colored. "There's a big difference, Seth. There really is."

Given the circumstances, her pointing it out was sorely offensive. His lips parted in exasperation. "You don't think I know that?"

Exhaling a whoosh of annoyed breath, she arched a thin, dark, perfectly tweezed eyebrow and challenged, "Do you?"

If he was honest, maybe not, but under the circumstances he hardly wanted Jenna enumerating his deficiencies in relationships with women or otherwise

probing his sensitive spots. For the first time, he silently damned her for knowing him well enough to
guess his Achilles' heel. The truth was, he really
didn't have much experience with women. Oh, he
loved sex, of course. That was a man's lifeblood as
far as Seth Spencer was concerned—an attitude
shared by all the Spencer men—but when it came to
mixing pleasure with emotion, Seth had always
avoided women. Until Jenna.

"I guess you *make love* to Dom?" he said now,
trying to keep his tone even. But when could Dom
and Jenna have gotten together, a voice in his mind
asked. And if what Jenna said was true and she was
getting married, why had she made love to Seth now?

Forget it, Seth thought. A relationship with Dom
simply couldn't have progressed to the point where
they were getting married. Seth had only left New
York six weeks ago! Besides, *he,* not Dom, had been
dating Jenna for the past year and a half. Sure, deep
down he'd wanted to head back to New York and
claim her, but Seth had known that was impractical.
He had a bank to run.

Yesterday, however, he'd begun considering calling Jenna in Manhattan, to see if she'd changed her
mind and might want to keep in touch with him. He'd
barely admitted it to himself at the time, but he'd been
considering suggesting that Jenna fly to Tyler for a
long weekend visit.... Seth hadn't been sure he should
take that risk, though.

And now Jenna was in Tyler. Just moments ago
she'd been half naked and lying across his desk, too,

and now Seth simply couldn't grasp what was happening. Had Jenna really said she was marrying Dom Milano?

She didn't bother to answer his question. He watched in stupefaction as she straightened her top, then he listened to the rustling fabric of tights as her endlessly long, showgirl legs scissored toward the door. As furious as he was, he had to admit he was affected by her graceful movements. She looked like she was dancing, not fleeing his office as if the hounds of hell were on her heels. When she turned, Seth was pleased to see her chin quivering. It was a show of weakness virtually unknown to Jenna, and while he wasn't proud of it, Seth hoped she was feeling even guiltier than that uncharacteristic tremor indicated, especially if she was really marrying Dom.

But she's not. She can't be. It's impossible. Besides, even if she was, why would she come all the way to Tyler. Once more Seth reminded himself that for the past year and a half she'd been dating *him,* not Dom, then pure fury whipped through him. Had Jenna been sleeping with Dom *while* she was seeing Seth?

He drew in a deep, steadying breath, but his mind continued to race. He had a million questions, but he was far too much of a man to make himself vulnerable. He just wished he couldn't so easily see Dom's appeal, but Dom was one of those sexy, swarthy Italians women always swooned over. He looked like a younger, taller Al Pacino, and he managed to share female interests without ever seeming unmasculine.

He was a clotheshorse, for instance, just like Jenna, and Dom could talk as enthusiastically about street rumbles he'd fought during his youth in Little Italy as he could about other things Jenna loved so dearly, such as art shows and foreign films.

Grinding his teeth, Seth had a flash fantasy in which Dom was translating Italian movie subtitles for Jenna in a seductive voice, and then Seth tried not to recall the knowing look in Dom's teasing, flashing dark eyes. Dom very definitely possessed the kind of challenging male gaze that promised a woman passion, and as he visualized that insinuating look, Seth's fingers curled, knotting into tight, angry fists.

"I'd prefer to keep the specifics of my relationship with Dom private," Jenna was saying stiffly from her place at the door. "But I—I thought you should, uh, at least know what was happening. Actually, Dom *insisted* you be told this. And...well, Seth, there's something else I really need to tell you now...."

"I've heard enough already," he growled under his breath, shoving his clenched hands deep into the pockets of his trousers, largely so she wouldn't see him fidget and realize how affected he was by this news. "Jenna," he continued, raising his voice but managing to keep it thoroughly controlled. "Let's stick with Dom for the moment. If you're marrying him, why didn't you bother to tell me when you waltzed into my office?"

"How could I? You didn't give me a chance!" she burst out, her voice still hoarse and tinged with arousal, the dark color that suffused her cheeks deepening to a guilty scarlet.

"You're right about that," he muttered, unable to take his eyes from her as he thrust a frustrated hand through his short dark hair. Gritting his teeth, he decided she had some nerve looking so damn gorgeous, standing against the door, so tall and slender, her scrap of a skirt topping those annoyingly long, luscious legs that had been wrapped around his waist just minutes ago, squeezing the breath out of him.

Seth bit back a groan. He'd missed her so much. Even now, her silken red-streaked hair looked too touchable, feathering against poreless cheeks that had been as smooth as water under his mouth. Her lips were swollen, berry-red and pleasantly bruised from the needy, insistent crush of his kisses. Despite the situation, looking at her made heat pool in his belly, filling him with ravenous lust all over again. He glanced at the desk, then blew out a murderous sigh.

"Okay," he forced himself to say, moving toward her, his mind whirling, his voice taking on a harder edge. "You're absolutely right, I didn't give you a chance to talk to me when you got here, but you didn't exactly complain about it, did you, Jenna?" Hadn't she come here for exactly what he'd given her? Hadn't she been going crazy without him? His mind still couldn't quite process what she'd said about Dom. "What did you expect me to do?" he bit out when she didn't respond, suddenly unable to contain his uncertainty any longer.

"Expect you to do?"

"Yes...when you come all the way here to Tyler and waltz into my office dressed like that."

She stared down, looking appalled. "Dressed like what?"

She knew what. Seth's lips parted in shock as his eyes drifted upward, over the sinfully short skirt, to the powdery lace top that so snugly cupped her full breasts. The collar wasn't fully buttoned, and even from here, Seth could see ample cleavage. No, he decided, it definitely wasn't his imagination. Jenna's outfit was calculated to drive a man wild. And it had worked.

She was surveying him with nonchalance that had to be feigned. "What happened is all my fault, I assume?"

As if I attacked her. "Since when is making love anybody's *fault?*" he couldn't help but challenge.

"We had *sex,*" she corrected.

"You seem committed to keeping that distinction clear," he muttered. No doubt, because she really intended to marry Dom. Realizing he was standing numbly in front of her, like a fool, Seth lifted a hand and leaned it against the door's molding, conscious of the fact—but hardly caring—that he'd trapped her against the wall. Warring emotions ripped through him as his gaze dropped, tracing the rose swell of breasts he'd just palmed and tortured with his tongue. Breasts, if the truth be told, he'd come to secretly think belonged to him. Dammit! Surely he'd heard her wrong. That, or he was neck-deep in denial. But he wasn't, was he? Earlier today hadn't Molly Blake said Jenna adored him?

"This is definitely your fault," he suddenly said, knowing he was contradicting himself, but unable to help it since befuddling his mind was only one of the many things Jenna Robinson did so well to him. "You damn well know how I react to tights with dark seams, high-heeled boots and leather miniskirts, Jen."

She swallowed hard, color flooded her cheeks, and as he curiously watched the pulse ticking in her neck, Seth was suddenly sure she'd worn the provocative clothes on purpose. Oh, yes, Jenna had had every intention of arousing him. Making love with her hadn't fully cured him of his desire, either, he thought angrily, his groin traitorously aching. But why the incredible claim she was marrying Dom Milano?

"When I dressed this morning, I wasn't thinking," she now defended with unnerving calm. Showing a spark of the usual Jenna, her glittering green eyes now settled on his, holding a dare. "But then, I didn't happen to pack anything made of burlap, Seth."

"Oh, don't worry," he returned dryly, still fighting denial about the abrupt, southward turn of their relationship. "Judging from that crowd you attracted on the sidewalk, tights with seams up the back go over well in Tyler." He arched an eyebrow. "Staying in town long? If you don't mind me asking, that is?"

"A few days," Jenna said, her low-pitched voice still stiff. "I came…to work with Molly Blake on the promotion for her new bed-and-breakfast."

That was rich. Before this, Jenna had never left

New York for freelance jobs. "Happy to have gotten the work for you."

"Thanks for the referral."

He eyed her. "Couldn't do the work by courier?"

Her mouth tightened. "No, it just so happens, I couldn't, Seth. Not this time. This job is special."

Seth didn't believe it. Jenna had done freelance art jobs for clients in far more desirable locales than Tyler, and she'd never bothered to leave home. No, Seth decided, relief flooding him, none of this made a lick of sense. She'd come to town expressly to see him, and maybe it was more her idea than she was admitting. "Dom?" he managed again, his eyes narrowing in challenge. "Did you really say you're marryir.g Dom Milano?"

Jenna nodded. "Yes, Dom."

She sounded so serious. But Dom was merely her friend. They'd been buddies for years. Besides, after Sue Ellis's divorce, it seemed obvious that Sue and Dom were getting together. Seth was usually as steady as a rock, but now he felt as if the floor were shifting under his feet. "Jenna," he couldn't help but say. "You're serious? You're getting married?"

Dangerous emotion sparked in her eyes. "I take it that surprises you?"

Seth could barely control his voice. "Hell, yes, it does."

The comment only seemed to rile her. "Why?"

His lips parted in astonishment and the roughly spoken words were out before he thought them through. "Because I shared your bed for the past a year and a half."

"Intermittently," she returned, her head now bobbing up and down as if this confirmed some opinion she'd privately held for some time. "And sharing my bed was fine for you. I see. But now there's something wrong with me marrying someone else?"

"No," he shot back, determined not to let her fluster him. "I guess not. Except for the fact that we just had some rather amazing sex on my desk."

"Sex," she said knowingly. "Is it really so hard to imagine a man wanting a *future* with me?" Her voice rose passionately as if they were now having exactly the conversation she'd anticipated. "Is it really so difficult to believe a man might *love* me?"

No. Of course not. He'd thought *he* loved her a few minutes ago, when she was still outside standing on the sidewalk. "Five minutes ago you seemed lovable enough," Seth admitted, unable to keep the huffiness from his tone. "So lovable, in fact, that if I was Dom, I'd be worried. Last I heard, faithfulness is usually an issue when it comes to marriage." Not that it had been with his mother.

Her eyes narrowed. "What would you know about marriage?"

"Not much," he admitted coolly.

Her tone was flat, her sigh long-suffering. "I would have told you, Seth. But as I mentioned before, you took me by surprise."

"I definitely took you," Seth agreed, his voice

dripping with innuendo, his penetrating gaze locking into hers like a hook.

"Seth," Jenna murmured in warning, looking afraid of what he'd do next. "The way you're looking at me…it's scaring me."

"Oh," he murmured, "I imagine I do look murderous at the moment."

"You do."

"Maybe you're right to be afraid," he volleyed, still livid as he glared down into the eyes he resented for being so heart-wrenchingly green, the bright color of glittering grass after a hard spring rain. "Why'd you breeze into town like this, Jen?" he suddenly found himself whispering, hoping she didn't notice his voice cracking under the weight of his suppressed feelings. Was it simply to hurt him? To reopen the wounds left by another two-timing woman—his mother? Before Jenna could answer, he continued, "And why'd you bring your wedding dress?"

Her lips parted. "The dress? How did you know…"

His eyes darkened, narrowing to slits, and he tried not to think about how gossip had affected him years ago when his mother left Tyler. "Everybody in Tyler knows you brought a wedding dress into town," he said flatly, hating her eyes again—now for the obvious emotion that filled them. Had she guessed he'd thought she wanted to wear that dress for him?

"You knew…?" she whispered.

"That you were marrying Dom? Of course not, Jenna. How could I? You didn't tell me until now."

"And so, you thought the dress was…?"

"A Halloween costume," he lied.

That remark seemed to eat at her. "Some people take marriage more seriously than that."

She'd hardly given him the chance to be one of them. Gaping at her, he edged closer, then wished he hadn't as the soft, powdery scent of her perfume swirled into his lungs, making warmth course through his body. His shirt had dampened, wilting against skin she'd left burning, and now he damned his own eyes for dropping hungrily to the lace top and barely covered breasts he wanted to touch again. When had she hooked up with Dom? As badly as he wanted to know, Seth wasn't about to give her the satisfaction of asking.

She was staring at him, clearly aware she'd been in the wrong to have sex with him, but nevertheless holding on to her composure. Oh, Jenna was good at this. He had to give her that. Only the uncharacteristic quiver in her voice suggested she might be experiencing some guilt. Reaching behind herself, she wrapped a hand tightly around the doorknob. "Well, I—I guess that's it, Seth. Dom wanted me to come. And I just needed to get this out of my system…to come here and tell you everything."

"Needed to get this out of your system?" he echoed, feeling more annoyed by the minute. "You're making this journey to Wisconsin sound like some sort of cathartic, spiritual quest."

She offered a quick, insincere smile, apparently unable to resist the bait. "If this was a TV show," she offered, "maybe I'd title it Pilgrimage of Peace. Or Mission of Mercy."

"And what would you be saving me from on this mission?" Seth growled.

"Not realizing what you missed."

So, she'd wanted him to see her one last time? She'd come here simply to flaunt her marriage? "What?" he managed to say, the defensive words seeming to come from outside himself. "Did you really think I'd care about any of this, Jenna?" Watching her strained expression freeze, he was half glad. Suddenly, he wanted to hurt her, just the way she was hurting him.

"Did I think you, Seth Spencer, would care?" she echoed lightly as if that were the world's most ludicrous possibility. "Of course not. You've never cared."

Nothing could be further from the truth. But didn't the good times they'd shared mean anything to her? What about the long weekend afternoons spent in bed in her Soho loft? Or their talks as they walked along the Hudson River? Or the late-night dinners in Chinatown? Seth frowned. When could she have spent time with Dom, anyway? It took everything he had not to demand an answer to the question. His voice turned steely. "Well," he forced himself to say dryly, "I can certainly see why you'd look askance on my care-giving skills."

She looked so surprised that if Seth didn't know better, he'd actually think she sounded hopeful. "You can?"

"Sure. Because I can see all the care you're lavishing on Dom."

Color flooded her cheeks, but to her credit, she didn't miss a beat. "Like I said, when I got here, you didn't give me the—"

"Chance?" Seth finished, his hand tightening around the door molding as, against his better judgment, he leaned closer. His lips were unwisely hovering above hers, and when he glanced down, he could see her knuckles turning white, then pink, where she gripped the doorknob.

And then he saw the engagement ring.

His lips parted slightly. His heart hammered. Despite the size and brilliance of the diamond, Seth knew exactly how he'd missed noticing it before now. He'd been too starstruck at seeing Jenna again, too intent on drinking in her features to observe minor details. But when he saw the ring, he realized Jenna's engagement really was a fait accompli. Warding off the feelings rushing through him, he dropped his voice a lazy notch. "Gee, Jenna, you really are getting married. And, like I said, I guess I somehow missed your protests when we were walking from this door—" he jerked his head "—to that desk."

Her voice was barely more than a contrite croak. "I already admitted it. I should have said something about Dom before…before…"

Obviously she couldn't get out the words. "Before…?" he goaded.

"Before—" She colored. "Before, you know."

He certainly did know. "Damn right you should

have said something.'' And now Seth supposed she'd need to say something about their lovemaking to Dom. As furious as he was, Seth figured Jenna's honest nature would demand it. But then, who knew for certain? Seth's mother sure had been duplicitous.

Their eyes met: Jenna's glittering green, his watchful brown. Suddenly, he wished he wasn't feeling her warm, mint-scented breath fanning his cheek or, when he looked down, not seeing how the plump, ripe swell of her breasts heaved with her agitation. After what they'd done on the desk, he should have been satisfied—any normal man would have been—but now an undeniable pang claimed his groin again. Leaning another breathless fraction toward Jenna's mouth, he fought the violent urge to kiss her.

She turned the doorknob, her eyes still riveted to his. ''I'd better go, Seth.''

He was still considering kissing her, but knew he shouldn't, not when he was in a near-rage at the idea of her marrying another man. *It's not an idea,* Seth mentally corrected. *It's a fact.* ''Don't let me detain you,'' he murmured.

For the briefest instant Jenna's armor dropped and she looked uncertain and confused, then the steely expression stole over her face again and she tugged the knob.

''Here,'' he offered. Reaching under her arm, he swiftly twisted the lock, then swung open the door for her. ''And, Jen?'' he said as she stepped across the threshold.

She turned, the artfulness of her profile and the soft,

fluttering sound of her voice nearly breaking his heart. "Yes?"

"If you need anything else while you're in town," he said right before forcing himself to shut the door, "make an appointment."

LUST HAD HIT her like a freight train, Jenna thought later that night. There was no other explanation for why she'd made love with Seth, except that his calling her "Jen" had rendered her as completely defenseless as the hard, possessive crush of his mouth. Even worse, she'd forgotten that Molly Blake had scheduled a meeting tomorrow between her and Seth, too. Hopefully, Jenna thought ironically, she'd be able to keep her fool blouse fastened at that time. *If Seth even shows.*

"Oh, Gretch," she murmured now, shifting the baby on her hip and cuddling her closer while pacing back and forth in their room at the Kelseys'. "You're the baby, so *you're* the one who's supposed to be crying, isn't that right?"

Nearly asleep, Gretchen merely snuggled in response. Her arms curled on Jenna's chest, elbows akimbo, while her tiny, pudgy hands folded beneath her like a bird's wings.

Jenna sniffled, brushing a tearstained cheek against flax-soft wisps of baby hair. She knew better than to cry over Seth, even if she couldn't stop herself. "I swore I wouldn't do this," she whispered softly. "What's wrong with me?" What happened to her well-intentioned plan to cruise inside the Tyler S&L,

drop her bombshell, then finish the work for Molly Blake and fly back to New York?

Ruefully pushing away the thoughts, Jenna gazed down, sighing as she continued lightly bouncing Gretchen. A few minutes ago, just as Jenna was snapping the baby into a yellow sleeper, Sue had called to check on them.

"When I phoned the gallery, Dom told me about your impromptu trip," she'd said, not put off in the least by Jenna's taking the baby to Tyler. "How did the munchkin behave on her first plane ride?"

"Wonderfully. She was definitely on her p's and q's," Jenna had reported proudly, smiling and thinking of how Gretchen had charmed the airline attendants. Jenna had wanted to tell Sue how everybody had assumed Gretchen was her daughter, and how much the flight had made Jenna look forward to motherhood, but that would mean sharing the news of her pregnancy, something she wanted to do when she and Dom jointly announced their marriage.

The art-buying trip to Paris was going well, Sue had assured Jenna before they'd hung up. "I can't believe you actually went to Tyler, though. What are you going to say to Seth?"

Jenna was still thinking about her pregnancy. "I really don't know, Sue."

"So, you haven't even seen him yet?"

"Not yet," Jenna had lied. She'd hated fibbing to her best friend, but what else *could* Jenna say? That she and Seth had made love on his desk today? Hardly. And even if she'd divulged that information,

Sue wouldn't have understood the implications since she didn't yet know about Jenna and Dom's engagement, and Jenna couldn't break her promise to Dom and confide in Sue. *What a mess.* Right about now, Jenna could use a girl friend.

"I completely forgot to tell her I borrowed the ring, too," Jenna murmured to Gretchen on an exasperated sigh, still wishing she could forget what had transpired at the bank. Yes, she wished lovemaking could be erased as easily as a chalk drawing on a blackboard, or painted away, like a scene from canvas. *If I'm lucky, I'll wake up tomorrow with amnesia.*

"Doubtful," she murmured. The image of her and Seth, half clothed and gliding across the top of that mahogany desk, was now indelibly imprinted in Jenna's mind. "Yep," she muttered, "the scene could have been burned onto my frontal lobes with a branding iron."

And how could she marry Dom after what she'd done?

"You have to!" She fought a rush of panic. The engagement wasn't yet official, but that hardly mattered. Dom had poured out his feelings when he proposed, and she deserved a stable life, one full of love for herself and the coming baby.

Nervously, Jenna toyed with the ring on her finger, thinking of the note she'd left perched precariously on the display case, saying she'd borrowed it, and then hoping Dom had rearranged the contents of the case, so the ring wouldn't be missed. Not that her taking it mattered; Seth hadn't even seemed to notice it. Which was just as well, Jenna decided now, feeling a twinge of guilt. Beyond having dinner to celebrate the inclusion of Antonio's artwork in the gallery, Seth had never paid any attention to it, so he wouldn't have recognized the ring, and deep down, Jenna really hadn't wanted to flaunt the faux diamond and hurt Seth.

"It *is* beautiful," she whispered, staring down at the ring. Set in gold, the cubic zircon shone brilliantly, catching light like a star. The ring was one of artist Antonio Juarez's signature pieces. An up-and-comer, the gem craftsman was making a name for himself by designing intricate filigree sets that held surprisingly inexpensive stones. Some even showcased chips of everyday glass from items as common as pop bottles.

The previous year, after a well-publicized robbery at a political luncheon in midtown Manhattan, the European trendsetter in costume jewelry had begun attracting high-rolling American clients, largely female members of the Manhattan elite who no longer felt comfortable wearing pricey, authentic jewelry around town. Antonio's decision to display his work at Soho Designs had been such a coup that Dom and Sue had treated Seth and Jenna to dinner at Elaine's on the company's expense account. Since then, even the mayor's wife had stopped into the gallery to buy a butterfly-inspired broach studded with ruby-colored stain-glass chips, and it was rumored that the purchaser of some dangle earrings had been an emissary for a member of English royalty.

"I'd better call Dom tomorrow," Jenna whispered, feeling homesick as she thought of the gallery. But should she tell him what happened with Seth? Wasn't she morally obligated to do so? *It didn't mean anything, though.*

It did to me, sounded a voice from deeper within her.

It was Seth who didn't care. She bit back a moan of frustration. Despite his lack of commitment, it was just like Seth to make love to her like that! Superficially, of course, he projected an unnerving air of suave self-possession. Everything from his painted silk ties to his hand-woven belts, to his professionally polished oxford shoes was kept in perfect, mint condition. She'd rarely seen his dark brown hair untrimmed, much less noticed lint on the fine fabrics from which his suits were tailor-made. Jenna suddenly frowned. No, before today, she'd never seen him wearing a shirt that looked so uncharacteristically rumpled and unstarched.

Well, in spite of his image, Seth was impulsive. Jenna had always suspected he possessed wild, untamed urges at which his lovemaking only hinted. Urges that left her wondering how a man could bury so much emotion. Not that Jenna was particularly outward herself. Still, what was Seth hiding? Why did she feel so sure that, behind his self-contained facade, he hid emotions so deep he was afraid to let them out? Was he the owner of feelings so powerful he secretly feared he'd be overwhelmed by them?

Or was that only Jenna's wishful thinking?

Seeking distraction, she took in Gretchen's relaxed, chubby body, and the china-blue, sparsely lashed eyes that were squeezed tightly shut. Lost to sleep, the baby looked as if she hadn't a care in the world. For an instant Jenna's worries lifted, and a smile curled the corners of her lips. In her mind's eye she saw herself pushing a stroller, changing a diaper, folding pink and blue sleepers. *Hard to believe I'm really going to be a mother.*

No sooner had she thought that than she swallowed hard, her throat aching. Why hadn't she told Seth about the pregnancy? Why hadn't she been able to force out the words...words she'd flown all the way across the country to say? How was she going to tell him about their baby now? He was going to be furious at how she'd withheld the information during their encounter today.

Feeling at a loss, Jenna glanced around the room, taking in the comfortable furnishings and soothing, blue-green color scheme. As she'd gabbed with Sue on the phone, she'd opened the curtains, and now, beyond her and Gretchen's reflections in the window, Jenna could see the quiet residential street. "Tyler, Wisconsin," she whispered, barely able to believe she was actually in the town Seth had spoken of so often.

It reminded her of her old hometown—and the loneliness of her childhood. It was so damnably quiet here. Too quiet. Everything inside her suddenly ached for Manhattan, and she wished she was in her Soho loft, listening to blaring taxi horns and raucous shouts from people carousing the clubs. Tyler's silent, still night, by contrast, threatened to coax out too many old feelings. Staring at a slice of golden moon and an array of stars that seemed to leap and dance over the silhouetted trees, Jenna found herself wondering exactly where Seth's house was…and what he was doing right now…and maybe, just maybe, if he was thinking about her.

But he wasn't!

Turning from the window, she swept her gaze over the wedding dress. It was draped over the bed, her sewing kit beside it. Hadn't she brought the dress to Tyler for the same reason she'd borrowed the ring—to make Seth jealous? Couldn't she admit that much? Hadn't she secretly hoped that she'd announce her marriage only to have Seth break down and tell her he had feelings for her? Of course no such thing had happened.

Sighing, Jenna kissed the baby's cool, smooth cheek. "Soon, you're going to have a little friend to play with," Jenna murmured, gingerly lifting Gretchen and placing her in the crib Johnny Kelsey had set up in the room's corner. For a long moment, Jenna stared into the crib, her hand creeping down to cup her still-flat belly, her eyes misting as she watched Sue's baby sleep. Then she headed for the bed. Sitting on the mattress, Jenna absently ran her hand over the wedding dress. Yesterday morning, while packing, she'd told herself that she had no choice but to bring it to Tyler, since it needed to be rehemmed before she married Dom next week, but now Jenna wished she'd left it at Soho Designs. Last year she and Sue had bought the dress in a second-hand shop, intending to use it for a store display. They'd both loved it so much that Jenna was sure Sue would want her to be married in it.

Married.

To Dom.

Steadfastly, she ignored the dread filling her, nervously wiggling the engagement ring on her finger again, unable to stop the unbidden fantasy that the ring was Seth's gift, one he'd given her as easily as he'd given her a baby.

"The baby I didn't mention."

Not that she didn't understand her own motives. She wasn't that self-deceptive. Regardless of the tone he'd taken at the bank, and even if she knew better than to entertain the idea, Jenna had wondered if he wasn't secretly harboring feelings for her. While it was true he'd abruptly left her in New York six weeks ago, Jenna had realized something else: once she told him about the pregnancy, she wouldn't be able to find out how he really felt about her.

Their relationship would change. One minute, they'd simply be Seth and Jenna. In the next, they'd be Seth and Jenna who were about to become parents. Even if they weren't going to raise their baby together, they'd have a bond. Now her heart pulled. It wasn't fair to Dom, but didn't she owe it to *herself* to wait and tell Seth? Shouldn't she try to talk to Seth more honestly tomorrow at Molly's and find out, once and for all, if he thought their relationship had any chance?

She groaned, then shook her head as if to clear it of confusion. Maybe if he hadn't called her Jen in that low, sexy voice of his, she'd have been able to say her piece and turn her back on him forever.

Impulsively, she gathered the wedding dress in her arms as well as the copy of *Women Who Love Too Much,* crossed the room, draped the dress over a chair, then absently disengaged the engagement ring when it snagged on the lace. No, she decided, returning to the bed again and whisking back the covers, tonight was definitely not the right night to hem the gown.

Damn her soul, but just for one more night she was going to keep dreaming about Seth Spencer.

MOMENTS BEFORE, when Sue Ellis breezed into Soho Designs, leaving a string of brass bells to clank against the door, Dom had been stunned. Now he thrust a hand through his jet hair, stared through the open door of the cluttered inner office they shared and eyed the uniformed police officer lounging in the gallery proper. Wincing, Dom decided that the evening light streaming inside was too bright. He preferred gray days, and that was especially true, given his current mood.

"Find the papers the cops wanted?" he asked.

"I haven't even started looking yet," Sue said.

As he pushed aside a stack of artists' portfolios, she hiked her jeans and her tall, thin body floated to the floor. She squatted in front of a file cabinet, and he leaned his backside against the edge of a metal desk, squinting at her and feeling determined to keep the hurt from his voice. "So, you weren't really in Paris?" he began dryly, keeping his voice low, since he didn't want the policeman to hear him.

Not that a love-spat was in the making. Sue shot him a quick smile, then continued absently rifling through the files. "Of course not, sweet knees."

Dom frowned. "You really didn't even go there?"

"Nope." As Sue located and pulled a sheaf of papers from the cabinet, her eyes darted toward the door. "Dom, you know I never go overseas on the spur of the moment." She shot him another smile as she pragmatically thrust the papers at him. Looking distracted, she pulled her long curly strawberry hair into a ponytail, secured it with a scrunchie, then quickly rose to her feet, dusting off her hands. "I can't believe this happened," she muttered under her breath. "When Antonio finds out that diamond ring's gone, he's going to be positively hysterical."

"I'm hysterical right now," Dom said grimly.

Sue sent him a dubious glance. "You're too obviously male to become hysterical, Dominick."

He sent her a lopsided smile. "That's what you think, Susan."

"That's what I know, Dominick."

Despite the circumstances, Dom couldn't help but broaden his smile. Glancing through the open door, he took in the uniformed man awaiting them in the next room. The officer, who'd introduced himself simply as McBeck, had said he'd prefer to wait for the arrival of the insurance investigator before he took Sue and Dom's statements.

"And we're right in the middle of changing shows," Dom murmured with a disheartened sigh. He shook his head ruefully, staring at the countless canvases stacked against the walls. Earlier this morning, before Dom had noticed the missing diamond, he'd been removing pictures by a Chilean watercolorist and hanging abstract oils. Now realizing his tool belt was still strapped over his jeans, he set aside the insurance papers Sue had handed him, took off the belt and tossed it to the desk. As he did so, his gaze returned to the next room, drifting over columned pedestals topped by sculptures, then lingering on the glass case where Antonio Juarez's costume jewelry had been displayed on black velvet. "Why does the guy always have to include one real gem in his collection?"

"It's his secret trademark," Sue said.

"Great," Dom muttered. "Why didn't you tell me?"

"Believe it or not, I forgot to. The ring was marked as Not For Sale, and it just slipped my mind."

"I knew something was wrong, when I noticed just one piece missing." He shot her a glance of censure. "And if I'd known you weren't really in Paris, we could have begun to straighten this out sooner."

"Well, I'm here now," she offered.

"How did the thief know what to take?"

Sue shrugged. "Must have been someone who knows about his special trademark."

"So you don't think it was just someone off the street?"

"Doubtful," she returned.

Dom's eyes softened as he looked at her, turning liquid black. Leaning, he lightly toed the door, so it swung partially shut, shielding them from Officer McBeck. When Dom lowered his voice, it carried a hint of seduction. "Now, what were you saying before?"

Sue's eyes, usually so clear and blue, were still narrowed with worry. Now they sparkled anyway. "I was saying that I know a few things about you, Dominick Milano."

"Like what?"

A grin claimed her mouth. "That I'm in love with you."

He chuckled softly. "Will you still love me if our gallery winds up going broke because of this theft?"

"Of course. But why do you always make everything so dire? We have insurance, Dom. So does Antonio."

"Hmm. If you were so in love with me," Dom continued, "you wouldn't have lied and said you were going to Paris on a buying trip. You would have taken advantage of having Jenna baby-sit, and you would have stayed in bed with me." He scrutinized her. "I know there's a cop out there now, and it's not the best time to talk, but did you need a break from me or—"

"No! Are you crazy?"

"Are you having second thoughts about us getting married?"

Her lips parted in astonishment. "Don't be silly."

"Then what…?"

Sue caught her lower lip between her teeth, worrying it. "I'm sorry," she suddenly gushed. "I know I should have told you what I was up to…" Glancing toward the half-shut door, she added, "Look, maybe you're right. Maybe we should talk about this after we file the police and insurance reports."

Dom shrugged. "The insurance guy isn't here yet, anyway."

"True, but…"

Tilting his head, Dom surveyed her a long moment. "Out with it," he said, his slight flicker of a smile meant to assure her he wasn't really angry. "I know you've always got some trick up your sleeve, Sue Ellis. What have you done this time?"

"Nothing really," Sue said pensively. Lifting a finger, she trailed it absently down the front of his shirt, a comfortable once-brown cotton pullover that had artfully faded to beige. "I just wanted Jenna to spend some time with Gretchen, that's all."

Dom frowned. "Jenna's with Gretchen all the time. We're like a family around here, have been for years."

Sue shrugged, glancing toward the door again and nervously retucking a white blouse into the waistband of her jeans, preparing to meet the investigator. "I know, sweetie. But I was thinking that if Jenna cared for Gretchen around the clock for a few days that she'd start to want a baby of her own.''

Dom stared, unable to catch her drift. ''Huh?''

''Well, if she realized how much she really wanted a baby, then I thought maybe she'd try to talk to Seth.''

Dom drew in a sharp breath. ''You were match-making?''

Sue stared at him. ''Don't you think I should?'' she began defensively. ''Jenna's my best friend. She's like a sister. You love her as much as I do. And she's wanted a baby with Seth from the moment she first laid eyes on him. Remember?''

When he'd mistakenly thought Sue was in Paris, the last thing Dom had considered was that she was trying to get Jenna and Seth back together. Now Dom could only shake his head. ''Remember what?''

Sue sent him a look of censure. ''Seth came in to buy that painting for his office, remember? And when he turned to go, Jenna said, 'What a hunk. I swear, I could have his baby.' Those were her exact words. I can't believe you don't remember it. You were standing right there, hanging the Keith Halstead show.'' She frowned. ''Or maybe it was the Guy Dean show. Anyway, the point is that leaving Gretchen with Jenna must have worked, because now Jenna's gone to Wisconsin.'' Looking suddenly pleased with herself, Sue's mouth quirked into a smile that warmed his heart.

''Well,'' Dom began diplomatically, wondering how to break his news and not wanting to burst her bubble. "I'm not entirely sure that's the only reason Jenna went to Wisconsin. There's something I really should confess to you, too."

Unfortunately Sue was no longer attending to him, but staring past a coatrack, umbrella stand and a box of Christmas decorations toward a dressmaker's model that had long stood in the corner of the office. "Am I going crazy or what?" she murmured. "I could have sworn that dress Jenna and I bought last year was on the model." She squinted at Dom. "Wasn't it, sweet knees?"

Turning, Dom stared at the model. "What dress?"

"That wedding dress, remember?"

Dom's heart missed a beat. Sue was right. The wedding dress had been draped over the dressmaker's model for a year, and he supposed he'd become so accustomed to seeing it that he hadn't noticed it was gone. His eyes trailed over the room's clutter. "I thought something around here was missing. I mean, besides the diamond."

Sue looked pleasantly surprised. "See?" she murmured, as if this was proof of a benevolent life force. "We might be having problems with this theft, but at least my plans for Jenna worked. She must have taken the dress to Tyler." Sue's hands settled on Dom's waist and she gazed up at him, her eyes turning misty. "Maybe she's asking Seth to marry her right now. Do you think he'll come to his senses and acknowledge his feelings for her?"

Dom couldn't help but wince. "I hope so."

"Wouldn't that be wonderful?" Sue gushed, her

blue eyes brightening with excitement. ''I called her earlier, but she said she hadn't talked to Seth yet. Maybe she did after our conversation. As much as I wanted to tell her about you and me getting married, I simply couldn't bring myself to, not when she's still so torn up about Seth's leaving town. But if she took the wedding dress to Tyler…''

Dom could only wonder how he'd gotten himself into this bind. ''Like I said, I've got a confession to make.''

Sue's eyes narrowed as he knew they would. They'd opened Soho Designs together years ago, before Sue had met her first husband or even thought about having Gretchen. ''What have you done this time, Dominick?''

''First, you know I love you, Sue.''

''Your confession's getting off to a lousy start,'' she said dryly, staring at him as if to indicate she was in no mood for sweettalk. ''You do realize a policeman is waiting for us and we've got an insurance investigator on the way. This is not the right time for you to announce that you've pulled one of those stunts for which you've become famous.''

''My confession can wait,'' he assured.

She gave him a rapid once-over, unable to help the mild flirtation in her eyes, then simply said, ''Now.''

''You know I love you,'' he repeated.

Sue didn't look the least bit moved. ''You said that already.''

''Words of love are always worth repeating,'' he returned. ''Don't you think?''

Her eyes had narrowed to tilted slits of blue. "Usually only when the lover's done something unconscionably bad."

He couldn't help but chuckle. "Admit it, Sue. You like me to be bad."

"Dominick," she warned.

Swiftly, he hooked a finger into the waistband of her jeans and tugged her forward, so her breasts cushioned against his chest as their hips locked. Without hesitation, he delivered a sound, thorough and very wet kiss, then pulled back just a fraction, so he could look into her eyes.

He was pleased to see Sue was trying not to smile. "C'mon, what did you do, Dominick?"

He winced. "I asked Jenna to marry me."

Sue's eyes widened like blue saucers. "Excuse me?"

Shaking his head rapidly, he held up a hand, indicating she shouldn't get the wrong idea. "I mean not really," he said.

"Marriage is an either-or proposition," Sue managed, "which means you asked her or you didn't—"

His hands tightened around her waist. "I had exactly the same idea you did," he assured quickly.

"Which was?"

"To get her and Seth back together. We've been listening to her talk about him for so long, and even if she won't admit it to herself, she's in love with him."

Sue could merely shake her head. "What did she say to this proposal?"

He nodded. "I didn't let her answer. You see, she's pregnant and—"

Sue's jaw dropped. "Pregnant?"

"She just found out. I walked in when she was getting her test results over the phone, and since I thought you were in Paris, I figured I'd offer to be a father to her child, but on one condition."

"That she go to Tyler and tell Seth about the baby?"

"You know me well."

Sue pressed a hand to her heart, then blinked back tears. "You're so sweet, so romantic. I admit it, I'm too overwhelmed to be mad, and I can't believe she's having a baby. She wants one desperately. She's going to be so happy."

Dom blew out a long sigh. "Not if the plan doesn't work and I have to tell her I can't give the baby a name, that I'm marrying you."

Sue sighed. "Ah, for what you've done, maybe I should back out and leave you to your fate with Jenna."

"I do love her," Dom admitted.

"But only as a friend," reminded Sue.

"True."

"It's going to work. I bet she calls later today, to tell us Seth proposed."

"Having Gretchen with her is bound to help," Dom admitted. "Seth adores her. Every time he's around the gallery, she winds up in his arms. He's a natural-born father, he's just never figured it out."

"Not yet, anyway," said Sue.

A knock sounded at the door. "Ms. Ellis?"

Sue raised her voice. "Yes, I'm in here with Mr. Milano."

"It's me. McBeck. The insurance investigator is here now."

After offering a soft, sly pat to Sue's backside, Dom opened the door. "I'm sorry we've been in here so long," he said to McBeck. "Sue and I had a tough time finding those insurance papers you wanted."

"About the artist, Mr. Juarez," said the investigator who introduced himself as Joby Marks. "Has he been informed of this?"

Dom bit back a smile. With his strapping body, red hair and red handlebar mustache, Joby Marks looked like a player out of an old Western film. He was wearing a white-pressed shirt and creased jeans.

Sue said, "I left a message for Antonio. He'll call back."

As Joby Marks delivered a number of rapid-fire questions, most of which Sue answered, Dom noticed a corner of paper sticking out from beneath Antonio Juarez's display case. Drats, Dom thought ruefully, he'd swept this place yesterday, but then, it was amazing the damage that customers could do. Tourists were the worst. When Joby Marks finally tugged on the end of his mustache and glanced around the gallery, Dom snapped back to attention. The investigator said, "You two have any employees?"

Sue shook her head. "Just Jenna."

Red eyebrows lifted. "That would be Jenna…?"

"Robinson. She's like family," assured Dom.

"Hmm. And where is this Jenna?"

This Jenna. That didn't sound good. "Tyler, Wisconsin," said Sue. "But—"

"I'm sure it's nothing," Joby Marks quickly said. "These are just routine questions."

For a second, it had seemed as if Joby were suggesting Jenna would steal from the gallery. "Jenna really is our best friend," Dom assured.

"Of course," the insurance investigator replied. He smiled. Eyes that had previously looked suspiciously red-brown, like a fox's, turned soft and benign in a way that brought Dom a rush of relief.

Chapter Four

So far, the meeting with Jenna had lasted only fifteen minutes, but every time Seth's gaze dropped over her snug, pink dress, that fifteen minutes started feeling like eternity. *If you need anything else while you're in town, make an appointment.* Yesterday, those had been his famous last words. Now, as he watched Jenna cross a partially furnished room in Molly Blake's Victorian home and unclasp her portfolio, Seth told himself he should have sent someone else from the bank to meet her. Hell, he definitely would have, if he'd realized Molly intended to leave them alone in a bedroom.

Gretchen wasn't around to help dispel the tension, either. Molly had left with her in tow, saying that her own four-year-old, Sara, wasn't about to miss this opportunity to pretend to be a mommy.

A mommy, Seth thought now, shaking his head and biting back an unexpected smile at the thought of Molly's little girl. Sara had huge blue eyes and a blond pageboy with bangs, and she was such a tiny thing that it was hard to imagine her, even twenty years in the future, starting her own family.

She must miss her daddy, Seth thought, recalling the man who'd made Molly a widow. Given how abruptly his own mother had left Tyler the year he was fourteen, Seth could definitely sympathize with the Blakes' loss, and he hoped he could justify giving them a loan, so they could turn this place into a bed-and-breakfast. But where had his own mother gone? he found himself wondering, unable to stop the intrusive thought. What had Violet Spencer done with her life? Was she still living? Wasn't there a possibility his mother had passed on?

Even now, after all these years, Seth had no way of knowing. A hell of a thing, he thought. Because his father, Elias, forbade it, Seth and his brothers had never searched for her. Quinn and Brady deserved better, Seth decided now, reflecting on his own youthful decision to willfully forget her. Yes, Quinn and Brady deserved to hear, from their mother's own lips, why she hadn't stayed in touch. Then came a deeper idea. *Maybe you do, too, Seth.*

Yeah, they all had a right to know. After all, Seth hadn't had any better luck than Quinn and Brady when it came to settling down and leading a normal life.

And now Jenna's marrying Dom.

Glancing abruptly away from her, Seth felt his heart squeeze in a way he'd prefer to ignore. It was strange, but despite his loss, he was beginning to want a family. The urge came from being in Tyler again, from spending time with Quinn and Brady in the Victorian on Maple Street where they'd grown up, a house, not unlike Molly Blake's, that had once been filled with love and laughter. For the umpteenth time Seth sighed, wishing he wasn't so conflicted. One minute, he was secretly dreaming of settling down; the next, he'd recall the hurt he felt after his mother left Tyler, and then he'd decide once more that he'd be a fool to give away his heart.

Not that it mattered, he admitted, shifting his attention to the one women in whom he'd ever been truly interested. She was still silently arranging artwork on the lone piece of furniture in the room—an iron double bed. Judging from her look-but-don't-touch demeanor she was thinking about the brief pleasures they'd shared on his desk—and trying to communicate nonverbally that she didn't want a repeat performance.

Seth did. Last night, as he'd tossed and turned, he'd even admitted how deeply his emotions were involved, something he hadn't completely understood until Jenna announced her marriage. He'd considered calling to talk her out of it, but he doubted his pleas would have any effect, since she'd obviously made up her mind. Nevertheless, he'd looked up the phone number for the Kelsey Boarding House, then he'd lain awake, conscious of the fact that Jenna was only blocks away and that the phone was just inches from his hand.

Now recalling their lovemaking on a rush of righteous anger, he thought, *If only Dom knew what the woman's been up to.* Suddenly feeling as if his body was wound tight with too much raw energy, Seth re-knotted the burgundy tie he'd worn with his best navy suit. Jenna, of course, had chosen to wear another sexy outfit calculated to undermine his bankerly composure. She was flaunting that rock of a diamond Dom had given her, too.

"As you can see from the drawings on the bed," she began now, her professional tone granting Seth the status of client, "the logo for Molly's bed-and-breakfast is going to be a red rose and yellow tulip twined around ivy."

As Seth edged dutifully toward the bed and peered over her shoulder at the drawings, he wished the spring-sweet floral perfume wafting his way wasn't making him want to bury his face so deeply into her neck. "The logo looks great, Jen," he found himself murmuring.

Although Jenna was keeping things all-business, he thought he heard a telltale catch in her voice. "You really like them, Seth?"

Nobody else could have done better. Emotion made his throat ache as he flashed on the past, on Jenna dressed in nothing but a silver silk nightie, bending over the drafting table in her loft, her green eyes narrowed in concentration so deep she'd forgotten he was even visiting. He couldn't keep the huskiness from his voice. "Didn't I always say—" He realized he was referring to their relationship in the past tense. "Don't I always say," he began again, "that you should quit the gallery? Start your own business?"

"Yes," she managed, her voice strained. "You've always said you have faith I could do more."

"I didn't just say it. I mean it, Jen."

Color flooded her cheeks as if she were remembering past conversations, so many of which had occurred in her bed. For an instant, her skin looked the exact same soft pink as the secondhand vintage sweater-dress she was wearing. Curve-hugging and feminine, it had a jewel-neck collar and turned-back cuffs, both of which were trimmed with tiny gray beads. A scandalously high hemline, loosely woven gray lace stockings, and an intricately tied blue-pink-and-gray silk scarf turned an otherwise goody-two-shoes confection into something that was pure Jenna Robinson.

She blinked her irresistible green eyes as if she'd just become aware of his dangerously close proximity, and as their gazes meshed and held, something in the sudden, pensive downturn of her mouth made him wonder if she wasn't struggling internally, wanting to say more about her marriage to Dom.

Seth guessed not, though, because all she said was, "Well, maybe one of these days I'll do more freelance work." Then she eyed him another moment, now almost as if she expected *him* to say something more intimate. But given the circumstances of her marriage, how could he? Suddenly realizing he was staring too hard at her moist, pink-lipsticked lips, he tried to avert his eyes and couldn't. His heart missed a beat. She was close…so close that in a second his mouth could cover hers.

Leave it to Jen to widen her eyes, seemingly registering exactly what he was thinking. He felt as transparent as glass. Just as he leaned a fraction, meaning to kiss her against his better judgment, she swallowed hard, brushed past him and strode across the room, heading for the relative safety of the mantel, her gray high heels clicking on the hardwood floor.

Maybe it was just wishful thinking, but she sounded unsettled by the near kiss, the usually low, husky voice that drove him half-mad now turning falsely bright. "Isn't this fireplace marvelous?"

He forced himself to avert his attention from her, to take in the carved wood and tile, wishing she hadn't reminded him of their joint enthusiasm for old architecture. "You'd like my new place," he murmured.

"Maybe I'll have a chance to see it," she said guardedly.

He nodded toward some exposed grout. "I take it Molly intends to replace the tiles?"

For a moment, Jenna actually seemed to forget the tension between them as she warmed to the topic of the bed-and-breakfast Molly wanted to open. "Yes. Molly's brilliant, you know. She's got so many incredible ideas for how to renovate. This place could be amazing, Seth. The name—the Breakfast Inn Bed—is adorable. And the neighborhood— Well, you grew up here, so I guess you already know it's called Ivy Lane—"

Despite his conflicted mood, Seth couldn't help but smile at the excited hitch in her voice. "So I hear."

"Well, it's quiet and prestigious, and I think with the right promotion, Molly can attract clients from larger cities. You know, people who are looking for a small-town getaway. Some of the ideas she's discussed with me will make it so romantic."

The only romance Seth really wanted to talk about right now was Jenna and Dom's, but keeping his mind on business, he prodded, "Romantic?"

Jenna nodded. She headed toward the bed again, but this time took a safe space opposite him. She leafed through drawings that depicted how the rooms would look once they were decorated. "See?" she murmured, lifting her gaze from the mattress to his eyes. "From the layout Molly sent me, I put together some sketches for you to look at. Molly wanted me to, so you could better imagine the bank's future investment. I guess she'll talk to you when we're done up here."

He eyed the drawings. "So far, so good."

"When the renovations are complete, Molly and Sara are going to be living on the third floor," Jenna continued. "The reception desk will be downstairs, of course." Her breath quickened. "Didn't you notice that staircase? Isn't the wood to die for? I think it would be great if Molly could match it, maybe even use it for the reception desk.

"I'm designing stationery and a registry book that will use an ivy, tulip and rose design. There's going to be a lovely sitting room downstairs with a fireplace, Victorian-style sofas and chairs. Nothing too fussy, though. Molly wants the place to stay homey.'' Jenna tapped her nail on another drawing. ''And look—''

Gazing down, Seth took in a sketch of an ornately decorated dining room with several tables and eye-catching high-backed chairs. ''Looks expensive,'' he murmured, wondering if the amount Molly had requested would cover the renovations.

''Oh,'' said Jenna predictably, as she often had in the past. ''You're a banker. What's money to you?''

He shot her a look of mock censure. ''I keep trying to tell you. Guys like me turn into bankers because we never spend our money.''

''Tightwad.''

''Ouch.''

Jenna didn't look the least perturbed. ''C'mon. Be honest. What do you think of the menus?''

Lifting two samples, he scrutinized them, then replaced them on the bed. ''They all look great.''

''Molly hasn't decided which to go with, but I love the idea of using the ivy-leaf border with a tulip and rose at the top.'' Jenna lowered her voice. ''You've got to give her the loan,'' she pressured. ''There's a place called Timberlake Lodge around here, which I hear has put Tyler on the map, so to speak. I really think this woman can make a go of an inn.''

He offered a long, sideways glance. ''So you're a banker now?'' he teased.

''No,'' she returned, challenge sparking in her eyes, ''but I know small towns, Seth.''

''I thought you hated them.''

For an instant, she looked undecided, then ventured, "Maybe not as much as I used to."

Before he could react to the missed beat of his heart at the idea that Jenna might adjust to small town life, she continued, "Each of the guest rooms up here on the second floor will be named after a quilt pattern. Apparently, there's a quilting circle that meets around here, at a place called Worthington House."

Seth couldn't help but chuckle. "I know those ladies well."

Jenna rose to the bait, smiling. "The acquaintance isn't favorable?"

He shook his head. "Martha Bauer has never forgiven me for stealing pumpkins out of her pumpkin patch. And Emma Finklebaum, whose about eighty now, once saw me streak naked through the town square. Not to mention the fact that my brother Quinn's been dropping by there lately—" He paused, his heart suddenly pulling as he realized he wanted Jenna to meet his father and brothers. "As near as I can tell, Quinn's about to become the quilting circle's first male member."

Jenna fought it, but she laughed. "A male member?"

Seth grinned. "You have such a dirty mind." Glancing at the bed and realizing they were heading exactly where they'd wound up yesterday, Seth added, "You haven't been here long, but it sure sounds as if you've been getting around town."

Relaxing, Jenna chuckled and Seth's whole body warmed. It had been six weeks too long since he'd

heard that soft, melodious sound. ''Getting around?''
she said dryly. ''It wouldn't take long to see the
sights. You could put Tyler under a microscope and
still miss it.''

He wanted to say he was glad she *hadn't* missed
it, glad she was here, but the words wouldn't come.
After all, she'd made it perfectly clear that she hadn't
come here of her own accord. She'd said Dom insisted Seth be told about the marriage, but why?

She glanced around the room. ''Molly intends to
get new furniture for all the rooms. All the beds will
be king size of course—''

Seth simply couldn't stop himself. ''No desks?''

She lifted her gaze again, and he was pleased to
see another smile flickering at the corners of her
mouth. ''Beds only. Desks need not apply.''

''Pity.''

''Seth,'' she returned in censure.

''Jenna,'' he said.

And then, before he knew it, he was on the move,
circling the bed. Stepping before her, he impulsively
placed a hand on her shoulder. The fuzzy soft fabric
of the ultra-feminine dress warmed his palm, just the
way the soft catch in her breath warmed his heart. ''I
think we need to do some more talking,'' he said. ''I
want some answers, Jenna.''

INADVERTENTLY, Jenna's hand drifted downward,
gliding over her belly. She knew it was wrong, but
she couldn't bring herself to tell Seth about the baby,

not yet, not when he might confuse his feelings about her and their pregnancy. "Answers?"

Something flinty touched his eyes, turning the liquid brown orbs a shade darker. "Yes, answers," he repeated, now looking frustrated, a flood of words following, as if he'd had them on his mind for some time. "Why'd you come waltzing into Tyler with your wedding dress, Jenna? Was it to try to hurt me? To make me jealous?"

"Of course not," she defended, though the truth in what he'd said ruffled her. He obviously didn't give an inch when it came to expressing his emotions, so she hated admitting he'd gotten so far under her skin. "I told you. I came to Tyler to finish up the work for Molly."

Seth hardly looked convinced. "And why does Dom think I should know about your marriage, anyway? And even if he did care, why couldn't you just pick up the phone and call?"

"He insisted I come here bodily."

Everything in his smoldering eyes reminded her of just how bodily their contact had been. He said, "Jenna, this just doesn't make any sense."

Unfortunately, she didn't think so either. "Well, that's the truth."

His eyes narrowed another fraction, and she wished she wasn't quite so conscious of him. Woodsy and male, his scent pulled through her nostrils and dovetailed into her lungs with her every breath. Huge and hot, the hand he'd forgotten was still curled around her shoulder, the thick fingers flexing, unconsciously stroking the fabric of her dress. Even worse, his lips were hovering directly above hers again, so warm and firm and inviting, just as they had been moments ago. She'd been so sure Seth wanted to kiss her. She'd throbbed from wanting it, if the truth be told, but why couldn't he admit he'd missed her, thought about her?

"Dom wanted you to come here?" he repeated.

She thought of the baby and swallowed hard. "Yes."

Another hint of anger stirred in the depths of those eyes that had always drawn her like a magnet, and Seth's voice suddenly lowered, turning into a low, gruff, accusatory whisper. "How long were you seeing him, Jen?"

Taken aback, her jaw slackened. "Excuse me?"

"You heard me. How long?"

Her heart hammered. Moments ago, Seth had been so congenial. But all that had vanished in a heartbeat. Now he was accusing her of two-timing. The accusation was so far off the mark that her defenses rose, snapping into place like a drawbridge. She gritted her teeth. If there was one thing she hated, it was being reminded of her extreme vulnerability where Seth Spencer was concerned. On a rush of pride, she found herself saying, "That's probably none of your business." Feeling the heat in her cheeks, she added, "You were in and out of my life, Seth. You came and went. Weeks went by when you never even called."

Only now realizing his hand was on her shoulder, he dropped it, leaving her skin tingling from the touch. "You didn't call, either," he reminded dryly.

"And I don't recall Jenna Robinson living in a male chauvinist universe."

She squinted. "Meaning?"

He blew out a sudden, murderous sigh. "Meaning you damn well know how to pick up a phone." Dragging a frustrated hand through his hair, he added the one, simple word, "When?"

She stared at him petulantly, his domineering tone, as usual, bringing out the very worst in her. "When what?"

His voice lowered another notch, now sounding almost lethal. "When did you start seeing Dom?"

Actually, she'd never really *seen* Dom. There'd been no movies, dinners or window shopping, and certainly no sex, at least not yet. "We've been friends for sixteen years, ever since I moved to New York."

"That's not what I asked."

"After you so abruptly left town." That wasn't exactly a lie.

He eyed her a long moment. "'So abruptly'?"

Wishing the heat and color in her cheeks would subside, she said, "Yes, abruptly. You'd been at my apartment nearly all weekend, then, out of the blue, right before you left, you paused at the door to say you were moving to Tyler."

"I always said I was moving to Tyler, Jenna."

She merely nodded. "Wham, bam, thank you, ma'am."

Looking not the least bit sorry, Seth shot her another long glance of censure. "Didn't take you long to replace me."

"What?" Pausing before anger got the best of her, she drew a deep breath and exhaled, valiantly trying to master emotions she'd kept pent-up for too long, but she simply couldn't. "You're beyond help," she huffed. "Did you expect me to pine away for you?"

"I don't know about pining. A phone call might have been nice."

"You're a banker. *You* know how to pick up a phone."

"What does Sue say about this, anyway?" he started in.

Admitting Sue didn't even know about the wedding would hint that the plans weren't nearly as final as Jenna had made them seem. She settled on saying, "Sue?"

"Ever since her divorce, it seemed as if Sue and Dom were getting closer. Does she have any idea that you two were—"

"You make it sound as if I stole a man right from under my best girl friend's nose!" Jenna suddenly exclaimed, her temper spiking. "I've known Sue as long as I've known Dom. I wouldn't do something like that to her! You know me better than that!"

His voice was cool and dangerously controlled. "I'm beginning to think I don't know you at all."

"What's that supposed to mean? You make me sound positively deceitful," she managed in a horrified whisper, hardly wanting to know how he'd react when he found out the information she was withholding from him. Not that she could tell him right now. No, the middle of a heated argument was probably no time to tell a man he was going to be a father. When Seth said nothing, she ventured, "You know, Seth, it's not as if you ever hinted at wanting something more with me."

He looked every bit as angry as she felt, and even worse, she couldn't help but think that anger suited him. His eyes were gorgeous and thunderous. His brows knitted above them, looking the same rich, dark, touchable brown as his hair, and somehow, seeing him so emotional suddenly got to her, making her heart ache.

He said, "We were sleeping together for a year and a half, Jenna."

His damnable attack was making everything inside her simultaneously jump with anxiety and hurt with longing. "Right up until you left town," she protested.

"Oh," he said, almost mockingly. "Were you lonely for a whole day? Did it take Dom that long to fly in from the wings?"

Thinking of the baby, she stoically said, "Dom's more of an angel than you know."

Unmasked jealousy flashed in Seth's eyes, but it only further roused her temper, since he had no real right to it, did he? He'd rejected her, hadn't he? "An angel?" scoffed Seth. "I'll bet he is."

She'd about had it. "Seth!" she burst out, knowing it was hopeless to control herself around this man. "I deserve to be loved! I deserve what's he's offering me! I'm thirty-four! I'm running out of time."

"I'm thirty-*seven*."

"But you don't want marriage. You don't want kids."

"How do you know what I want?"

"I know because you said so. It was just sex between us, remember? A fun time between two consenting adults."

"That's what *you* wanted, Jenna."

He was so wrong. Heartbreakingly, painfully wrong. She'd wanted more. Sometimes she'd lain awake at night, needing him beside her and wishing she had the nerve to call him, but fearing it was too soon to see him again. She'd been terrified he'd think of her as too weak, too needy. He was so controlled, so strong....

But she'd desperately wanted more. She simply didn't know how to ask or to risk herself emotionally. What if he rejected her? Turned his back? Growing up the way she had, she'd gotten used to feeling love would never come her way, and she couldn't withstand any more raw, painful feelings of consuming rejection. For the briefest second, his voice turned soft. "That's what you wanted."

"Maybe I changed my mind," she ventured.

"*Obviously,* you changed your mind." Seth's eyes, now furious, dropped to her ring.

She fought it, but tears were welling in her eyes. "What do you want from me?" she managed to say, her voice breaking.

"Maybe I wanted a chance."

"I gave you over a year's worth of chances," she returned. And then, feeling she couldn't stand to let

Seth Spencer see her shed tears over him, she whirled around and fled from the room.

"DAMN THAT ROCK on her finger," Seth muttered. He could swear the diamond got bigger every time he looked at it. He glanced over the countless sketches Jenna had left on the bed, noting once more how talented she was, then he stared through the window, shaking his head in frustration and thrusting a hand angrily through his already mussed hair as he watched her head for the Cadillac sedan, Gretchen in tow. Anger had resurfaced from beneath whatever vulnerability he'd glimpsed a moment ago, and now Jenna was standing on the sidewalk, her expression murderous as she waited for Tisha Olsen to drive by, so she could cross the street.

Seth's frown deepened, and he squinted, leaning closer to the window, so he could get a better look at the white compact car parked directly behind Jenna. The cars were bumper-to-bumper, though there were countless other parking spots on the street. "Who's he?" Seth wondered aloud, scrutinizing the driver. Even after years in New York, Seth knew most people in Tyler. Not this guy, though. He was big, built like a football player, and he had a red handlebar mustache. He was wearing a leather bomber jacket, and since a coffee cup and doughnut box were on the dashboard, Seth figured he'd been parked behind Jenna for some time.

"Weird," Seth muttered, since the guy looked as if he were on a stakeout.

As she drove past, Tisha rolled down her window and shouted something to Molly, who was in the yard with Sara.

Molly yelled back and waved.

"Great." Seth emitted another angry sigh. Even from here, he could see a couple of women stopped on the sidewalk, curiously scrutinizing Jenna's outfit. One pointed at the gold Cadillac sedan, which a teller at the bank had, for some unknown reason, dubbed the Go-go-gold Mobile, a name that seemed to be sticking. Jenna had been in Tyler less than three days, but every citizen knew who she was. Even worse, they'd gotten a sense of the spark that kept igniting every time Seth and Jenna crossed paths. No doubt, they were gossiping about it.

"That," he muttered, "or they're saying how sad it is that the Spencer men can never keep their women." Even as he said it, he acknowledged that he thought of Jenna as his. No matter how many times he repeated the words to himself, the idea that she was marrying Dom just wouldn't sink in. It still had absolutely no reality. Like a hundred-degree day to an Eskimo, it seemed strangely distant, academic and abstract.

He tried not to recall the rustling whispers sounding behind his back after she'd left the bank yesterday. Every teller on the floor had taken one look at Jenna's face and registered exactly what had happened. How, Seth didn't know. He regularly took clients into his office and consulted behind closed doors. But Jenna was different.

He'd left work with the feeling that he might as well have broadcasted his sex life over the local radio. He swallowed hard. People knew she was marrying another man, too. Yes, the worst damn thing was how everybody knew she'd only come here to flaunt her marriage. Oh, he'd had enough pride to ignore Molly Blake's shy look of apology when he'd arrived at her house, but obviously, since their conversation at the bank, Molly had realized Seth wasn't Jenna's intended, after all. If Molly knew, then so did every citizen in Tyler.

But maybe Jenna won't get married. Despite the ring on her finger and the fact that she'd arrived in town toting a wedding dress, there'd been no mistaking the anger she'd expressed over Seth's previous lack of commitment. *I gave you over a year's worth of chances,* she said. Seth didn't quite trust it, but he could swear tears had been welling in the eyes of the usually invulnerable Jenna, too. Why couldn't women be more like banks? he wondered with a sigh. If Jenna were an S&L, he could charge right in, assess the situation and do whatever was required to shape reality to his liking. But what *did* he want from Jenna?

She was right. He hadn't given their relationship a chance. He'd even lied and said his mother was dead. That's how emotionally distant he'd been. At the time, Seth had assured himself it was a simple lie, a white lie. A lie for Jenna's benefit. Didn't *he* hate it when women acted as if a date was a forum where they were supposed to pull skeletons from their family closets, dust them off and present them as a way of fostering closeness? Besides, what man really wanted to share his past history?

Why had he really lied, though? And what had it cost him? How much distance had he really placed between himself and Jenna?

"And who *is* that guy?" Seth said once more. It was a crazy, fleeting thought, but he had the uncomfortable premonition that the redheaded fellow in the white compact had been waiting for Jenna. He started his engine, and as Jenna pulled out behind Tisha, the man slowly followed. Seth didn't like the looks of it. Hairs prickled at his nape. Shaking off the sensation, Seth assured himself he was merely rattled. He was overgeneralizing his emotions. His jealousy over Dom was spreading like wildfire to every man around, even this stranger in Tyler. Shaking his head, he reminded himself that he was used to New York crime rates. Nothing even remotely suspicious ever happened in Tyler.

Except, of course, Jenna's arrival.

No matter what she claimed, Seth couldn't believe she'd come here only because Dom had told her to do so. There was more to this. Not that he'd find out what, unless Jenna stayed and continued working with Molly. Seth turned toward the door, hearing Molly and Sara coming up the stairs.

Molly peeked inside the room just as Sara bounded toward him. "Ready to talk to me about the renovations?" she asked brightly, her relieved eyes passing over the drawings Jenna had left on the bed. "Jenna said you liked our ideas. She said everything went fine.''

He couldn't help but smile. Despite Jenna's fury at him, she'd retained her usual self-containment when she'd spoken to Molly. No matter what, Jenna was always the consummate professional. ''I'm impressed with the work you've been doing together,'' Seth said honestly. ''I loved the drawings.'' After a moment's pause, he added, ''I just wish Jenna were staying in town a few more days. I might be able to get a stronger sense of the other promotional materials you two have discussed.''

''If she isn't already planning to stay,'' said Molly, ''I'm sure I can talk her into it.''

Seth smiled. ''Thanks.'' Hopefully Jenna really might stay in Tyler a few more days. He'd never felt so relieved.

Chapter Five

"Thanks," Jenna said. She grinned as Caroline Benning lifted a well-fed, wiggling Gretchen from the high chair wedged between the two women, then she glanced around the dining room, wishing dinner at the Kelseys' wasn't a reminder that she hadn't been born into a big, rambunctious family. The sheer homeyness of the boarding house made her heart ache tonight. Johnny and Anna Kelsey's daughter, Glenna, had shown up, bringing both a chocolate mousse cake and her rough-and-tumble husband, an arson investigator named Lee. Pat and Pam Kelsey, whom Jenna had met when she'd checked in, had arrived with their son, Jeremy, too, and it did Jenna good to watch the family interact. Deep down, if she were honest, wasn't this the kind of lifestyle she really wanted? Hadn't she fled Bear Creek—not because she hated it—but because she felt unloved by her parents?

Soon, she thought, slipping a hand over her belly, she'd be starting her own family, and yet she already knew she and Dom would never duplicate the energy the Kelsey clan exhibited. Somehow she doubted she and Dom would ever have other children. If they even married. Were either of them realistically willing to commit before working out a physical relationship? Wasn't it possible that Dom had reacted too swiftly to the news of her pregnancy, just as her rush to say yes and get things settled was motivated by fear about raising the baby by herself in the city? If Dom really loved her, wouldn't he have let her know before now, despite her involvement with Seth? Or wouldn't he have proposed right after Seth left New York?

Dom and I never even talked about our marriage, she admitted silently. She'd been so glad to know she wouldn't be raising a baby alone in the city that she'd pushed aside her reservations, not seriously envisioning a life with Dom. She'd known him such a long time, she'd thought. Didn't that mean things would work out?

The next thing she knew, he'd been hustling her onto a plane to Wisconsin while she clutched Gretchen, the book, *Women Who Love Too Much,* and tried to convince herself she could easily get over Seth. Before now she'd never thought of Dom as anything more than the brother she'd never had, just as she'd thought of Sue as her surrogate sister.

Shaking her head to clear it of confusion, Jenna took in the Kelseys again. They seemed so loud and boisterous, passionate and interesting. Strangely, this evening with them was softening her, making her yearn for the small-town life she'd once fled. That, or she was merely reexperiencing the unwanted emotions she'd felt as she fled Molly Blake's today.

Throughout dinner the Kelseys had kept all the guests on the edge of their seats by regaling them with lively tales of intriguing town folklore, even offering an insider's account of an old arson at the locally famous Ingall's Farm & Machinery plant, a crime that Glenna's husband, Lee, had admirably solved.

"See? Before she came to Tyler, I bet Jenna was under the mistaken delusion that nothing ever happened outside the big city," Johnny Kelsey had teased.

Jenna had nodded agreement, thinking of Seth. "Oh," she'd assured, "this town is truly wearing me out."

"Next thing you know," remarked Johnny, "you'll want to buy a ranch outside of town. Isn't that what all you city folks wind up doing?"

Jenna looked thoughtful. "Trade in my fishnets for chaps? Now there's an idea."

"Do you want to hold her?" Caroline asked now, speaking of Gretchen.

Jenna smiled. "No, you go ahead."

"It was so much fun to help feed her." Caroline offered a soft, tentative chuckle as she caught Jenna's eye. "I love kids. Soon, I guess I'm off to *serve* the food," she added amiably, referring to the fact that she was working tonight at Marge's Diner. "I'm rarely called upon to literally shovel in the grub, so to speak. This was a first."

Jenna laughed her appreciation, reaching over the high chair to tug playfully at Gretchen's food-smeared play shirt. "The word *grub* definitely applies. Looks like my favorite munchkin entirely missed her bib."

Caroline didn't respond immediately. She wasn't quick to converse, so Jenna was glad she'd had the opportunity to further try and get to know her during dinner. In fact, Caroline was just the sort of person to whom Jenna was drawn; like Seth Spencer, she was complex and hard to figure out. A willowy, green-eyed, all-American beauty with light brown, sun-streaked hair, Caroline seemed as if she'd be the out-going type, at least at first glance. As near as Jenna could tell, though, Caroline wasn't an ex-cheerleader or majorette, and something in her eyes seemed overly aware, her demeanor too watchfully composed. Not that Jenna didn't trust her. She was obviously a sweetheart. Besides, countless times Gretchen had proven she possessed the world's finest-honed instincts when it came to a grown-up's character, and she'd taken to Caroline like construction paper to glue.

"Good for you," Jenna complimented as the plates were being cleared from the dining room, "you've definitely managed to procure the Gretchen Ellis stamp of approval."

"Yeah, it does seem as if she likes me." Happily bouncing Gretchen, Caroline dipped a clean paper napkin into a water glass and dabbed at Gretchen's lips. "And you liked those peas, too, didn't you, Gretchen?"

"The Kelseys will never serve peas again," Jenna said dryly. It had taken her, Caroline, and probably an act of God to stop the baby from flinging every last pea at Johnny Kelsey. Even worse, the old man had gleefully encouraged the bad behavior. Now, sensing Jenna's amusement, Gretchen giggled proudly, looking thoroughly pleased with herself.

Jenna winced. ''I need to get her out of that outfit.''

''She could use a bath.'' Caroline shrugged, adding, ''What did you do today?''

Jenna sighed. It was so nice to be asked that question. Usually, at this time of day, she was rushing from work, picking up take-out food, heading home from the gallery to face her empty loft apartment and wondering if she should break down and call Seth if he hadn't left a message on her machine. Sadness twisted inside her. Loneliness was such a lousy emotion. The worst. While she was growing up, her parents would often focus during dinner on their plans for the evening. If the conversation involved Jenna at all, it was to find out which baby-sitter she'd prefer. One thing she'd always loved about New York was being ceaselessly surrounded by throngs of people.

''Oh…'' Her breath suddenly caught. ''Sorry, Caroline. I completely spaced out for a minute. My mind was a million miles away.''

''It happens,'' Caroline returned with understanding.

''Today I met Seth Spencer over at Molly Blake's,'' Jenna explained, now half expecting Johnny Kelsey, who was listening, to start teasing her again about working for the competition.

''Seth Spencer?'' queried Caroline, sounding oddly

curious. "Isn't he the guy who just moved here to take over the Savings and Loan?"

Jenna nodded, an unexpected rush of pride welling in her over Seth's accomplishments, despite how confused, exposed and unaccountably angry she'd felt today. Oh, she knew the emotion wouldn't be appreciated by Seth, despite how he'd sounded today, but sometimes she felt as if he belonged to her. How could she help it? She was thirty-four and attractive, and she'd dated countless men, but she'd never wound up staying with any them. Somehow, it had never worked out. But with Seth…

Sharing a year and a half with him had seemed incredibly significant. And now his child was growing inside her. She was still barely able to believe she'd be a mother this time next year. Realizing Caroline was still watching her, she swallowed hard. "I met Seth when he was living in New York."

"Really? Did you know him well?" Caroline asked in an uncharacteristically chatty tone. "You must have, since he hooked you up with Molly Blake."

For the briefest second, Jenna was plagued by the fleeting sense that Caroline was fishing for information about Seth, but then she wrote off the feeling. "I know him fairly well," she admitted. *What an understatement.*

"Fairly?" Caroline echoed.

Jenna hardly wanted to elaborate. Fortunately, Johnny Kelsey spoke up. "Know Seth well?" he said. "Looks to me like Jenna's got that banker in her pocket. Yes siree, like I said, she's probably only staying in our humble boarding house so she can spy on us.'' Chuckling, Johnny pushed his chair back from the table, unabashedly patting his stomach. ''Yep. Molly Blake may have gotten our advice already but now she wants the real scoop on how to run a bed-and-breakfast, so she sent you over to take notes,'' he accused.

''Especially on the menus. Molly told me to pay extra attention at mealtime. I'll be happy to report that your wife's cooking is definitely a trade secret.'' Jenna grinned, glancing once more over what was left of the homey meat-and-potato meal. As full as she was, her mouth suddenly watered for the few rolls that remained in a warmer basket. ''I was hoping I'd find the recipe for those rolls on a microchip I could steal,'' she confessed in a hushed, conspiratorial whisper. ''Have one handy?''

Johnny clucked his tongue. ''Did you hear that?'' he called to his wife. ''Our supposed guests are really spies, smuggling out your recipes, Anna Kelsey.''

Jenna nodded gravely. ''In Gretchen's diapers,'' she assured darkly.

''Then you're passing both the secrets *and* the baby to the banker,'' returned Johnny. ''I see.''

''You got it,'' Jenna agreed, even though hearing the words *secret* and *baby* in the same sentence rattled her cage. It was crazy, but she was beginning to suspect that Tyler's citizens knew more about her secrets than they'd ever let on. Cringing, she recalled the heat in her cheeks as she'd slid off Seth's desk, righted her clothes and left his office. Yes, it was easy enough to imagine curious bank tellers calling the quilting circle members at Worthington House, who'd probably called the Kelseys...

Already, judging from the low-voiced, one-sided phone conversations she'd overheard emanating from Anna Kelsey's kitchen, there was some buzz about Jenna's arrival in town. Did people want to know why she'd spent time with Seth while planning to marry another man? Were they going to ask how Seth figured into the Jenna-Dom picture? Jenna blinked, assuring herself she was merely getting paranoid. Probably, those bank tellers had plenty of work to do and hadn't even noticed all the time she'd spent in Seth's office. She was hardly the center of the universe. People never thought about others as much as one supposed. Still, thinking of the time she'd spent on his desk made her blush. Her pulse quickened.

"Speaking of the devil," Johnny Kelsey suddenly said.

Jenna, whose eyes had settled on Gretchen again, jerked her head toward the door. "Seth?" Feeling suddenly, strangely ungrounded, she wondered what on earth he was doing here. After she'd stormed out of Molly's place, he was the last person she expected to see. Just looking at him made her heart ache, too. His broad shoulders filled the doorway, and even in casual clothes—he was wearing stone-washed jeans and a navy pea coat—that calm, self-contained bankerly air still clung to him. Even when he was explosively angry, he managed to communicate that annoying level of self-mastery. When he leaned, resting the portfolio case she'd left at Molly's against the wall, her throat tightened. It was nice of him to bring it to the Kelseys'.

Seth extended his greetings to all at the table, but his eyes never left Jenna. He said to Johnny, "I was hoping you'd let her out for a walk."

Johnny looked at Jenna, then back at Seth. "You look like bad news to me, Seth Spencer. If it was one of my own daughters, I'd probably say no."

"All your daughters are married," Seth replied mildly.

"And I think I'm old enough to decide for myself whether I go out, and with whom," Jenna put in, regaining her equilibrium and wondering if Seth had only come here to return the portfolio.

A second later, though, his lips curled slightly upward in a bemused smile and his eyes lowered, dropping appreciatively over the pink dress she was still wearing. "Does that mean you're getting your coat or not?"

Why did he have to be so damnably challenging? She wanted to hear what he had to say, yes. But his tone was so dictatorial that she was half-inclined to decline the invitation, just on the basis of that. Not that she could. Everybody in the room seemed determined to take the decision out of her hands. Caroline and Anna were already splitting up responsibilities for caring for Gretchen, with Caroline promising to quickly bathe her before heading to work at Marge's Diner and Anna saying she'd put her to bed.

"We won't be gone that long," Jenna protested.

"But we might," Seth countered just as Pam, who just happened to be coming from the hallway, arrived with Jenna's coat, saying, "Here. I grabbed it off the coatrack for you."

The next thing Jenna knew, she was alone with Seth on the Kelseys' front porch, sucking down a lungful of crisp October air and surveying the dark, velvet sky, a sliver of glowing moon and a smattering of twinkling stars.

Turning, she eyed Seth with suspicion, wondering if she should apologize for today, and wondering what she'd say if she did so, since her emotions regarding Seth were so confused. "Mind divulging where you're taking me?"

His eyes narrowed in the kind of challenge to which she'd long become accustomed. "Only if you're nice."

She shot him a sideways glance. "Nice?"

"Nice," he returned with husky promise. His slow, sensuous smile left no doubt as to just *how* nice he wanted her to be.

"YOUR HOUSE IS wonderful," Jenna said enthusiastically an hour later. As they walked toward the town square, her mind was reeling with the fact that Seth had not only shown her his home, but had taken her to meet his father. "Since Dad's house just so happens to be on the same street as mine," Seth had explained, his casual tone barely masking his anticipation. Already, Jenna had told him how much she'd enjoyed Elias's company, not to mention that of his brothers, who'd been visiting.

Seth raised an eyebrow. "You really like the new house?"

"Yeah. You sound surprised."

He shrugged. "It's not exactly your style, Jenna."

"Oh," she said, keeping her tone light and not really expecting a response. "I've got a style?"

His eyes flickered over her outfit. "You've got plenty."

She smiled. Neither of them had mentioned their earlier, heated exchange, and now Jenna didn't want to, since spending time with him was turning out to be so pleasant. Pushing her hands deep into the pockets of her leather coat, she sighed deeply, her breath fogging the cool night air. "Actually, I think your new house is great, Seth."

"I don't know," he protested. "It seems...too big."

She chuckled. "You do need some furniture."

He shrugged. "You know I'm not much for decorating."

She was. That was the difficult thing, she thought, her heart pulling again. She and Seth were such complementary opposites. One look at the new, four-bedroom house on Maple Street, and she'd known exactly how to transform it. It wasn't the kind of place in which she'd expected Seth to live, but then nothing in Tyler vaguely resembled anything they'd known in Manhattan.

Drawing in another deep breath of cool, clean air,

her eyes strayed from the tall trees in the town square to the softly lit porches down a side street, most of which were decorated with inventively carved jack-o'-lanterns. No, this place was a world away from New York City, and Seth's house was the sort a man bought only if he was thinking about raising a family.

Somehow that hurt. He'd bought a four-bedroom house, and after a year-and-a-half courtship, hadn't asked her to move in with him. All the empty rooms seemed to beg for people to fill them, too. Even worse, one would be perfect for a nursery, and Seth's old furniture from New York kept reminding her of being in that city with him. Just seeing his king-size bed brought back a flood of memories.

"Definitely a family place," she finally offered.

"I guess it is," he returned, sounding thoughtful.

Perfect for kids. The previous owners had left a bricked-in sandbox in the backyard along with a swing set and a shed that Jenna imagined had once been filled with badminton nets, croquet sets and bicycles. A white-picket fence, like something out of a middle-class dream, surrounded the yard, and the wide front porch had plenty of space for both a porch swing and lawn furniture. "I like the porch," she said, speaking her thoughts aloud.

"Yeah?"

She nodded. "It'd make a great conversational sitting area. You could get a standard indoor-outdoor rug, maybe in black..." She chuckled softly, feeling pleased with herself. "Black would be perfect. And you could use a black wrought-iron sofa and chairs, but with all-weather cushions, printed in mismatched animal prints.''

He looked amused as they crossed the street, heading into the square. ''Animal prints, huh?''

She visualized the fabrics. ''Leopard spots, zebra and tiger stripes.'' She smiled. ''You've got to admit, it would be the wildest-looking front porch in Tyler.''

''Think they'd tar and feather me, and send me out of town?''

''Maybe simply put you in stockades in the town square,'' she returned amiably, suddenly fighting a guilty flush. It was one thing to wax philosophical about how Molly Blake could transform her home, but should she be mentally redecorating Seth's house?

Maybe I wanted a chance, he'd said.

The words he'd spoken today were haunting her as they entered the town square. A chance. Was that why he'd come for her tonight? Did he want to formally resume their relationship? If so, it was time to tell him about the baby. But how would he feel?

He was watching her carefully. ''Mind?'' he asked, sliding one of his huge hands over a lapel, then inside the pea jacket.

She shook her head as he took out a cigar, then watched as he struck a match and lit it.

''That's one thing I always liked about you, Jenna,'' he murmured.

''What?''

''You're the only woman I ever met who can stand the smell of a good cigar.''

Chuckling softly, she drew a deep breath, catching

a whiff of the smoke as it curled past her. "I do like it, actually," she confessed, even though he already knew that. "Except in enclosed spaces." Otherwise, the smoke seemed to meld into the deep, dark velvet of the night. "It smells like winter," she said.

"Hmm." He nodded into the trees. "Mind cutting through the town square?"

"Figured we would." As it had turned out, only seven blocks lay between his house and the Kelseys'.

As they stepped from the sidewalk, she sighed again, feeling the soft grass beneath the soles of her shoes. The grass was turning brown, one of many signs that a harsh Wisconsin winter was on the way. Leaves had been raked into piles under the trees, and their orange and red colors were vibrant even in the dark. In just a few more weeks, the leaves would be completely gone, exposing the bare branches of the trees, and the ground would be covered with a soft, endless blanket of snow. She suddenly frowned, drawn from her reverie. "What?"

Seth stilled his steps, shook his head and glanced over his shoulder. He shrugged. "I don't know."

Her lips twitched as a revelation struck. "Are you having trouble adapting to life outside the big city?"

Shooting her a sideways glance, he still looked pre-occupied. "Huh?"

"You keep looking over your shoulder, even though I doubt there's much crime in Tyler, Wisconsin," she explained. Leaning into him with an impulsive laugh, she bumped against him, meaning to jar him out of his concern. "Do you think somebody's following us? Spies, maybe?'' Her laughter deepened, becoming throatier as she recalled how much she loved to tease him. ''Yes, that's it, isn't it? Everybody knows I'm stealing trade secrets from the Kelseys so Molly can beat out the competition, and now Johnny Kelsey's sent people to counterattack.''

Rolling his eyes, Seth drew on his cigar and jerked his head toward a park bench. ''Feel like sitting?''

''Sure.''

Despite the fact that it was a standard green park bench, she wound up seated right next to him. It felt good, too: the damp autumn air cooled her cheeks while the warmth of Seth's big body shielded her from the wind. For a few moments, the silence was broken only by the sound of rustling leaves. Light from the stars and moon and a distant streetlamp were barely enough to illuminate Seth's face, but she could see his patrician profile: the strong, square jaw, his watchful eyes, the sudden, pensive downturn of his mouth. Six weeks ago she'd been convinced she'd never see that face again.

''Why'd you come to the Kelseys' tonight, Seth?'' she asked, tired of feeling the question burning inside her. She wanted to ask him other things, too, but she didn't have the nerve: Why had he seemed so anxious to show her his town? His home? To introduce her to his father and brothers?

He eyed her, his brown eyes narrowed, serious-looking in the darkness. ''I wanted to talk to you.''

''Well, shoot.''

He shrugged, glancing around. ''Sitting on this

park bench…'' He paused, searching for the words. ''I don't know, Jen. Hell, this is weird. I feel like we're on a good, old-fashioned, all-American date.''

Before now, they'd spent a lot of their shared time in bed. She agreed, saying, ''A far cry from New York, huh?''

Jointly mulling over those memories, they both stared from the bench toward some leaves that swirled with a gust of night breeze. A lump formed unexpectedly in her throat. ''It's nice,'' Jenna suddenly managed. ''Sitting on a park bench, I mean.''

Tilting back his head, he glanced up to where bright stars twinkled through the lace canopy of darkly silhouetted leaves. ''Smells good out here, huh?''

She drew another deep breath. ''You don't miss the scent of gasoline and diesel?'' she teased softly, sending him a sideways smile. ''The scent of exhaust from seven million cars?''

Seth shook his head. ''Not nearly as much as the scent of all that trash when the garbage guys go on strike.''

There were other things, too, though, and now Jenna felt a sudden wave of homesickness for the smells of cakes from the Italian bakeries, and of strong coffee from Turkish cafés. Her voice lowered to a rasp. ''Do you miss it, Seth?''

When his eyes caught hers, she could swear he wanted to say he missed her. ''A little.'' He glanced around. ''But I'm here to stay.'' Suddenly reaching, he glided his palm over the back of a hand she'd rested on her thigh, and his larger fingers curled over hers. "I came to the Kelseys' tonight because I wanted to apologize…to tell you I'm sorry about how abruptly I left the city. I know…" He glanced away a moment before his eyes sought hers again. "I know things have changed…"

She wanted to protest and say she wasn't marrying Dom, but she knew she had to move on with her life. Unless Seth declared feelings for her—and not under duress—she needed to marry Dom, had to. She wanted this baby to have a father, so she didn't say anything.

Lifting his hand from hers, Seth stretched an arm behind her, resting it along the ledge of the park bench. "I have trouble getting close to people, Jenna," he finally said, his eyes not meeting hers, but now tracing those endless piles of autumn leaves. "I guess I just wanted you to know that whatever happened between us in New York—" He smiled ruefully. "Or didn't happen between us," he added. "It wasn't your fault. You said you always felt your folks weren't as attentive as they should have been. And…" He paused once more, emitting an abrupt, frustrated sigh as if the words had gotten too difficult. "And I'm just sorry I didn't know how to be what you needed."

He hadn't been, not really. It was true, and yet her heart was hammering, her lips opening in denial. She had to fight not to protest. She wanted to lie and say he was being too hard on himself, that he was wrong. She compromised. "It's okay, Seth."

"Dammit, Jenna." He shook his head. "It's not okay and you know it. I didn't want to get close. I even lied about my family."

She frowned, her eyes lifting to his. She'd met his family tonight. How had he lied? "Your family?"

"I said my mother was dead."

Her eyes widened and her lips parted in astonishment. Seth Spencer would never cease to amaze her. "She's not?" She gasped. "Why would you lie about such a thing?" She couldn't believe it.

Seth shook his head. "I don't know. For all I know, maybe she really is dead. The truth is that I don't know what happened to her. None of us do."

Shifting her weight so she could face him, Jenna stared, her lips parting in astonishment. "What on earth are you talking about, Seth?" Nothing more than looking at him right now did dangerous things to her resolve to marry Dom. Seth looked so uncharacteristically open and vulnerable that it shaved a good ten years off his age. She felt she was glimpsing the little boy he'd once been.

"Not too long after we moved here," he admitted with a sigh, "my mother ran off with some guy. Ray Bennedict, that was his name. As it turned out, she'd been having an affair with him while we were living in New York. When Dad brought us to Wisconsin, he didn't realize she was having an affair, much less that the move would break up the relationship. Anyway, I guess Mom had to make a choice."

"And she ran away with Ray?"

Seth nodded. "We never heard from her again."

In Seth's voice she could hear the edge of bitterness. She could tell that grief and anger had tempered over the years, too, mixing with sadness and confusion. Her brow knitted with confusion. "How old were you?"

"Fourteen."

Suddenly, she realized what her coming here to announce an engagement must have done to him. Deep in his mind, Seth must have assumed that she, like his mother, had been having an affair with another man all along. She could barely trust herself to speak. "You were fourteen?" she repeated. He'd said it as if he were old enough that the abrupt loss of his mother shouldn't have bothered him. "That's so young."

He scoffed. "I was nearly in high school, Jenna."

She shrugged. "I wish you'd told me," she returned. "You could have, you know. I told you a lot about my parents and about how miserable I felt growing up in Bear Creek."

He drew thoughtfully on his cigar, then glanced her way. Just as surely as he'd opened the topic, he closed it by merely nodding affirmation. Then he said, "Cold?"

She shook her head, wishing he'd share more of himself and his emotions, and yet savoring the small piece of himself he'd allowed her to see. "No. The air feels good."

He dropped his hand to her shoulder anyway, wrapping strong fingers around her shoulder with slight pressure, urging her to lean against his side. Somehow her cheek wound up pressed against his chest. She was sitting there, utterly immobile and wishing this moment would never end, when she felt his body tense.

Startled, she began to stand, but his hand only tightened around her shoulder in warning, urging her to remain still. "What?" she whispered.

Seth's dark eyes were riveted to a nearby cluster of trees, and his voice was a low, barely audible whisper. "There's somebody out there."

She wanted to deny it, but Seth's concern was palpable, as real and tangibly hard as concrete. Fear slid through her veins. Freezing against him, she tried to tell herself that he was just unaccountably anxious, that they were both overly accustomed to well-lit, crowded sidewalks and a constant stream of city noise. Yes, they simply weren't used to dark, countrified parks, and the silence here was so unerringly deep that, last night, Jenna could have signed a sworn affidavit saying nothing could penetrate it. Now she scarcely heard her own whisper. "You're just paranoid. This is Tyler. There's nothing out there."

"The hell it's nothing," Seth said under his breath, his eyes studying the tree line. His upper body barely moved as he handed her his cigar. "Here. Take this."

"Don't go," she managed, even as her fingers molded around the cigar. For the first time, she realized how much fear she'd come to live with in New York City. Daily tabloids screamed headlines for horrible crimes. People bumped and crushed each other while subway signs offered explicit warnings to citi-

zens about how to watch their wallets and pocket-
books. Before this moment, Jenna had never deeply
thought about it. She'd accepted the fear just as she
had high rents and token hikes.

Now the fears she'd learned to carry with her were
acute. "Don't go out there," she repeated, suddenly
realizing she'd die if anything ever happened to Seth
Spencer. "Please, Seth."

Seth didn't even look at her. "Stay right here."

"Why do you have to be such a *man?*" she protested.

"I was born that way," he whispered.

And then he was gone.

ADRENALINE RACED through him. His heart pounded.
He couldn't even feel the weight of his own body as
it flew across the town square. As he shot like a bullet
toward the presence in the trees, he felt he was speed-
ing faster than light. And yet time seemed to slow.
Everything was heightened, sharper and brighter in
the dark. Running, Seth could make out countless fine
details in his peripheral vision: a squirrel sensing danger, sitting up on its haunches. A crow tensing, ready
to take flight.

Seth wasn't crazy. He'd definitely seen someone.
The whole time he'd talked to Jenna, a shadow had
been flitting behind tree trunks.

There! He saw something now!

Kicking up dirt clods and grass, he rushed into a
thicket of trees. He'd flush out the person. Force who-

ever it was into the open ground surrounding the town square's gazebo.

A dark figure streaked from between two trees.

He knew it! Even from here, he could see it was the same guy who'd followed Jenna from Molly Blake's house earlier. Seth cursed under his breath, and then he gave his all, running full-out, propelled by the knowledge that any man who intended to lay a hand on Jenna Robinson should start begging now. Because Seth intended to show no mercy.

Chapter Six

"Calm down," Jenna urged in a hushed tone once she and Seth were seated inside Marge's Diner. "You look like you're about to implode."

"Calm down?" Seth echoed, squinting in disbelief and uttering a soft curse under his breath. "We didn't even catch that guy, Jen."

The redhead had been too damn fast. Just moments after Jenna joined the chase, he'd disappeared down the alleyway across from Marge's. Winded, Jenna and Seth had stopped in the middle of Main Street, panting and holding their aching sides. Seth had kissed her then. Breathless, he'd leaned into her so quickly that she hadn't even seen him coming, his cool lips locking onto hers. Long ago she'd learned to expect the blissful searing heat that followed as his tongue swept inside her mouth, the sweet touch of his lips bringing such tantalizing promise that a shiver had raced down her spine.

Then, some blocks away, the white car had zipped across an intersection, and they'd rushed inside

Marge's to phone the police. Now Jenna sighed. "Well, whoever he was, we *almost* got him, Seth."

"I told you to stay put, Jenna," he reminded grimly.

She gasped a protest as she wiggled out of her leather coat, her cheeks still damp and flushed with the moist, autumn air. "Stay put?" she returned. "What do I look like to you, Seth Spencer? A dog?"

He tilted his head, considering. "Poodle?" he mused. "Maltese?"

"Pit bull if you're not careful," she assured.

His eyes narrowed with a returning hint of playfulness. "Hold your tongue, Jen."

"See. I knew it. You *do* think I can be ordered around."

Glancing through the windows of the diner, he searched the street as if he expected to see the white car; he no longer looked amused. "Of course I don't. You know better."

"Oh, sure," she countered, a faint smile now twitching at her lips since she'd never seen Seth so riled. "Stay put. Sit. Hold this cigar. The next thing you know, you'll be trying to command me to fetch, lie down and roll over."

It wasn't meant to carry an innuendo, but the words hung in the air, bringing smoldering heat back into Seth's dark eyes. He arched an eyebrow. "Lie down and roll over?"

She couldn't help but smirk. "Don't look so hopeful."

"Any man would."

He seemed to be thinking of Dom. "Maybe. But your panting-puppy-dog expression ruins your big-bad-banker image."

"Don't push me right now," he warned. "I'm really worried about seeing that guy again."

"Sorry. Until you need me, I'll just sit right here, fold my hands prayerfully and behave. I won't say a word, Seth. I promise." Determined not to further react to his endlessly annoying provocation, Jenna snuggled back in the red vinyl of a high-backed booth and glanced from the steamy plate-glass windows to the interior of Tyler's favorite hotspot. Unbelievable, she thought. She'd barely spent two days in town and she could pick out familiar faces in the crowd already: Caroline was waiting on their table, Seth's brother, Quinn, was at the counter, drinking after-dinner coffee and reading the *Tyler Citizen*, and Molly Blake, who was treating her daughter, Sara, to a hamburger and fries, was facing Jenna from the next booth.

"Really, Jenna," Seth started in again as he shrugged out of his pea coat and stretched a long arm to hook it on a coatrack. "I really wish you hadn't chased that guy."

"I had mace in my pocket," Jenna defended.

Seth sighed, thrusting a hand through his hair, looking faintly exasperated. "Good point," he finally conceded. "But you could have gotten hurt."

"Me? What about you?"

To his credit, Seth looked determined not to say something sexist. He shook his head. "You ruined a good Havana cigar,'' he finally grumbled. ''Believe me, that's my only real concern.''

''Havana's a big place,'' she offered lightly. ''I'm sure they'll make more.''

Her banter was starting to loosen him up. He scrutinized her closely. ''You really carry mace, Jen?''

She shrugged. ''New York City's dangerous.''

''And you're a dangerous woman.''

The way he said it made her heart beat double time. Right now she was definitely carrying a dangerous secret, one that was going to change the way Seth Spencer saw the world. She just wished the right moment would present itself, so she could tell him he'd soon be a daddy.

Suddenly, as if now reliving the chase scene through the town square, he blew out another murderous sigh. ''New York really *is* dangerous, Jenna. Maybe you should move.''

What? she thought. To a place like Tyler? Was he fishing for her reaction to the town? Quickly, she tamped down unwanted emotions, wishing she had never seen his homey, four-bedroom house, then she glanced toward a pay phone, from which Seth had called the police. ''Well, I can see the cops in Tyler are just about as responsive as they are in the Big Apple.''

Seth paused to nod his appreciation at Caroline Benning as she placed cups of cocoa on the table. ''Thanks,'' he murmured as Jenna and the other woman exchanged smiles, then he resumed addressing Jenna, "I just don't understand it. I know Brick Bauer. And Cooper Night Hawk's a good guy."

She shrugged, feeling sure Seth was overreacting. "They really didn't want us to come give a statement?"

Seth sipped the cocoa and shook his head. "Cooper sounded more worried about some felon who's on the loose from upstate."

"It's probably nothing," returned Jenna. "Maybe that redheaded guy wasn't even watching us. Maybe he was just passing through the town square and got scared when we chased him. Maybe we misunderstood."

Setting down his cocoa mug, Seth toyed with the edge of a paper napkin. "No. Like I said before, I saw that guy follow you from Molly's, Jenna. He was in a white car."

Frowning, she worried her lower lip, hoping he was wrong. "Are you sure? Did you get a good look at him?"

Seth blew out a sigh. "Good enough, I think. At Molly's, I was watching him from the window, but I could see his hair and mustache. And, like I said, the car was white."

"He had a mustache?"

Seth nodded. "Tonight, I couldn't tell. But the guy outside Molly's did."

Jenna hardly wanted to think a strange man was following her, and she didn't know anyone meeting the description Seth had offered. "If he's been following me, I haven't been aware of it." But would she? She'd been so busy thinking about Seth that she was half convinced an armed robbery could occur without her noticing. She shut her eyes briefly, thinking back over the time she'd spent in Tyler. "No. I know I haven't seen him."

"He's definitely not from around here," Seth supplied.

Jenna sighed. "If I'd just gotten closer..."

Looking glad she hadn't, Seth tersely said, "Given the taxes my family pays in this town, you'd really think Brick and Cooper would move on this."

Despite being worried for herself and touched by Seth's concern, Jenna couldn't help but bite back a smile. To hear Seth tell it, an all-points bulletin was in order, but it wasn't the right time to tease him. If he wanted to hear bloodhounds and sirens coming to her rescue, she could only silently enjoy it. Softening her voice, she said, "He was just some guy in a park, Seth. The police know what they're doing."

"But who was he?" Seth returned. After a moment, his eyes widened. "Wait a minute. Dom knows you're here. He *told* you to come to Tyler, right?"

"Seth!" She couldn't believe what he was implying. "I don't think Dom—"

"Do you think he hired someone to follow you?" Seth cut in, his eyes narrowing. "Did you see anybody on the plane? Think hard, Jen."

"Seth..." She almost chuckled. Calm, cool Seth Spencer seemed to be losing his usual control—and all over her. She couldn't believe he was accusing Dom.

''Think,'' he said again.

Sipping her cocoa and savoring the warm, sweet taste, she shut her eyes obediently, now visualizing the plane. There were the attendants who'd fussed over Gretchen, a man who'd helped her lift a carry-on into the overhead compartment. Finally she shook her head. ''There'd be no missing a man like the one you described. I caught a glimpse of him, but you got a better look. You said he was big, like a football player, and had red hair and a red handlebar mustache, right?''

''I think it was a handlebar mustache. It seemed like it at the time. But honestly, I'm not positive. He was in his car...''

She hated hearing Seth sound so uncertain. It was out of character for him. Finishing her cocoa, she shrugged. ''Well, the important thing is that he's gone,'' she offered.

Seth didn't look the least bit convinced. His pique returned. ''What if he's some guy from New York? Or from Madison? Maybe he looked at you and—''

''Decided to follow me? A complete stranger?'' Now she was starting to get exasperated. ''Admittedly, men can be animals, Seth, but I really don't think I'm being stalked by a man who saw me in an airport.''

Seth rolled his unusually alert eyes. ''Far worse things have happened to women.''

Jenna uttered a incredulous chuckle. ''With those words ringing in my ears, I'll certainly sleep better tonight, Seth.''

Fortunately, before Seth could inquire about the quality of the dead bolts at the Kelsey Boarding House, his brother Quinn appeared at their table, and then before Quinn could speak, Bea Ferguson from the Worthington House quilting circle sidled up.

"You poor woman! And right here in Tyler!" Bea exclaimed, having apparently already heard the story of the chase through the park. Placing a hand over her heart, Bea gasped. "It's a good thing a man was with you!"

Jenna took in the woman who looked to be in her late sixties. "Yes," she couldn't help but enthuse, fighting another smile. "Seth's quite the protector. You should have seen him with his teeth bared, furiously rushing at that—"

Seth lightly kicked her under the table.

"And you," continued Bea, turning to Quinn who, with his light brown, sun-streaked hair and green eyes, didn't look nearly as much like his brother as Jenna would have expected.

Quinn grinned at the older woman so flirtatiously that she became flustered, and Jenna couldn't help but imagine that Mrs. Ferguson's knees had weakened and that nothing more than support stockings were holding her up. Quinn chuckled. "Me, Ms. Bea?"

"Yes, you, young man," continued Bea Ferguson, blushing. "When are you going to find a nice, sweet woman to protect?" A light seemed to flash in Bea's mind. "What about Molly Blake?" she suddenly suggested. "She's been so alone since the loss of her husband." A smile flickered at the corner of her lips as if she'd just resolved Quinn's problems. "Yes, indeed," she enthused. "I think Molly Blake would be the perfect woman for you. And she has the cutest little girl I've ever seen."

"Kids?" Quinn's grin widened. "Are you crazy?"

Bea looked stern. "What's wrong with kids?"

"Children only complicate your life and take up time. I'm always on the go. I'll leave raising the little rugrats to other people."

What if Seth has that kind of reaction? Just as the thought registered in her mind, Jenna locked eyes with a very embarrassed Molly Blake, who'd overheard the callous remark and was cringing. Even though she was in the next booth, Quinn hadn't noticed her, and now Jenna prayed he wouldn't. Fortunately, her daughter, Sara, hadn't heard anything, since she was playing near the counter.

By the time Jenna averted her eyes from Molly's, Bea and Quinn were heading toward the cash register. "Be right there to ring you two out," called Caroline over her shoulder as she placed a cup of cocoa near Molly's plate. Glancing between Jenna and Caroline, Molly smiled her appreciation, mouthing "Thanks."

"Your brother just put his foot in it," remarked Jenna.

Seth was still worrying over the redheaded man, no doubt still convinced he was stalking Jenna. "Hmm?"

She nodded, telling him that Molly was seated behind him, and Seth winced. He glanced over his shoulder. "As much as I like my little brother, you know he's a total jerk, right, Molly?"

Recovering, Molly chuckled. "He's not looking for a date, anyway."

"Believe me," assured Seth. "You deserve better."

She shrugged. "Not all men like kids, you know."

When Seth turned back around, the words were out before Jenna thought them through. "Do you?"

Seth still looked lost in his own thoughts. "What?"

"Like kids?"

He considered, toying with the handle of his now-empty cocoa mug and chewing on the inside of his cheek. After a long moment, he sighed. "I don't know what I think anymore, Jenna. The truth is, after my mother took off, I think I decided that any women I ever got close to would wind up leaving me."

He eyed her a long, steady moment, his dark brown eyes looking almost amber in the warm light of the restaurant, and suddenly she felt sure he was thinking about her marrying Dom. When she arrived here, announcing her wedding, it really must have seemed to Seth like a self-fulfilling prophecy, given his own past history. His mother's leaving must have hit him hard, too. Otherwise, he never would have lied about her death. "Seth, look," she suddenly began, "I'm sorry—"

"No," he said, interrupting her, his gaze turning hard. "It's fair of you to ask that question, given the fact that we were close before you decided to marry Dom—"

"Seth, I—" She paused, her heart clutching, the words catching in her throat. Was she really prepared to say she couldn't go through with it? Was she really so in love with Seth that she'd rather be alone, even if things didn't work out between them?

He held up a staying hand. "Honestly, I never imagined myself marrying. And kids? I guess I've always felt pretty much like Quinn. Kids never really crossed my mind, either."

The hard implacable expression seemed to make clear that his attitude wasn't changing any time soon. His attitude was positively anti-parenthood. *Oh, Lord,* Jenna thought, simply gaping at him. *What am I supposed to do now?*

"DOM…" GRIPPING the phone tightly in one hand, Jenna flung a suitcase on the bed, opened it and began transferring folded stacks of clothes from the chest of drawers. "I'm so glad I reached you," she said in a rush, not letting Dom get a word in edgewise, since she was still running on panic over how Seth had all but announced he never wanted children. "I just thought you should know I'm on the next plane from Wisconsin."

Dom sounded relieved. "You told Seth, then?"

"Uh, that I'm pregnant with his baby?" Jenna swallowed hard, dropping a jewelry bag into the suitcase and coiling her fingers anxiously around the phone cord. Glancing toward the crib where Gretchen was soundly sleeping, Jenna reminded herself that she knew plenty of very strong women. Sue was raising a child without a father, after all. And if Sue could do it, Jenna could forget Seth, marry Dom, and settle for a comfortable, if not passionate life.

So, why did she feel so confused? Her heart hammered. She loved Dom, she really did, and she didn't want to lie to him, especially since she valued honesty in relationships, but she simply couldn't tell Seth about the baby, not after he'd leveled her with that last steely gaze. Since he didn't want children, shouldn't she forget about her promise to Dom and head out of town? It seemed the kindest thing to do. Wasn't it better if Seth remained none the wiser? Wouldn't his knowing just complicate matters for her and Dom? Or make Seth feel obligated to her? Suddenly, she blinked. "Did you say something, Dom?"

"You *did* tell him, didn't you, Jenna?"

"Uh, yes. Yes. I told him about the baby."

Dom didn't sound completely convinced. "And then he said…?"

"Just that he didn't mind you raising his son or daughter. He wanted to wish us all the luck in the world. Yes, that's what he said. Isn't that sweet?" Since Dom had sounded worried, she tried to reassure him. "As a matter of fact, Seth just treated me to a cup of cocoa at the most delightful little place called Marge's Diner—"

"Delightful?" Dom cut in, his voice hitching. "So you like it there? Tyler's a cute town, huh?"

Feeling relieved, Jenna realized Dom was probably feeling threatened by her earlier relationship with Seth. It was only natural. If anybody knew how much she'd pined for Tyler's native son, it was Dom. "Tyler's fine *for a visit,*" she emphasized for Dom's sake, even though her heart was secretly aching for the kind of lifestyle Seth had found. "But I'll be glad to get on the plane. When I left Seth, he was still worrying over what to get us for a wedding gift." There was such a long pause that she finally prompted, "He was asking me about silver patterns. Do you happen to have any in mind? I know silver patterns are supposed to be a girl-thing, Dom, but to tell you the truth, I'm clueless." This time, the pause seemed to stretch into eternity. "Dom? Are you there, Dom?"

His voice sounded oddly strangled. "I'm here, Jenna. But…"

But nothing, she thought. She'd already begun packing again, and was now doing her level best to ignore the moon and stars shining through the window. Somehow the silent, serene night itself seemed to hurt her. Seth's house was so damnably close, under this same soft, velvet sky, only seven easily walkable blocks away.

"Dom, are you okay?" she managed.

"Fine."

"You're not having second thoughts, are you?" The already panicked beat of her heart speeded. "Right now," she continued, speaking honestly, "I really need you, Dom. I feel so alone. More than ever, with the baby coming, I need to know I'm not doing this all by myself." Unbidden, she thought of Nancy and Ralph Robinson, who'd loved her in their own way, but who hadn't been there for her when she'd

needed them. The night of her emergency appendec-
tomy flashed through her mind, of how they were still
out bowling when her stomach started to hurt, and of
how the baby-sitter wouldn't listen to her, because she
was busy, talking to a boyfriend on the phone. A lump
lodged in Jenna's throat. "You have no idea how
much your proposal meant, Dom. Or maybe you do.
You know me so well, but I never knew you loved
me. I— Oh, God, you're *not* having second thoughts,
are you?"

There was another unnerving pause. "Uh, no."

But this near silence wasn't the least bit like Dom.
He usually talked a million miles a minute. "Look,"
she managed, her mind flying back to Seth's steely
gaze. "I'll see you tomorrow. My flight gets in at
around two, which means I'd better finish packing.
It's getting late here." Saying that, she managed to
ring off, and then began to wedge a pacifier, a rattle
and a children's book next to some of her clothes.
"Sue's going to be so glad to see Gretchen," Jenna
murmured, knowing how much Sue hated being sep-
arated from her daughter when business demanded it.
Suddenly, Jenna realized she'd been too upset to ask
Dom about their best friend. Was Sue back from
Paris?

Jenna's frown deepened. And why hadn't Dom
kept Gretchen in New York? Why had he been so
adamant about Jenna's bringing the baby to Tyler?
He'd said he had to hang a new show, but he'd often
done so when Gretchen was in the gallery.

Jenna shook her head to clear it of confusion—only

to have images of Seth quickly fill it again. If anything convinced her to leave town, it was his hot, delicious kiss in the street. He'd smelled like a thicket of North Carolina evergreens on the darkest coldest winter night. He'd smelled exactly the way Ralph Robinson had smelled when he'd taken walks in the woods with Jenna years ago, before Jenna realized he didn't love her as much as she needed him to. By the seventh grade, when she figured out the math, she'd been hardly surprised to discover that her parents married because of the pregnancy. They loved her, of course, but deep down, they hadn't wanted kids any more than Seth Spencer seemed to. No, Jenna wasn't the least inclined to have her own pregnancy pressure Seth into a relationship with her, which he otherwise didn't want. Not that it mattered now, given how he felt about children.

Jenna pushed away the thoughts, grabbing her toiletries and dropping them into a side pocket of the suitcase, then she suddenly gasped. Her heart pounded rapidly, slamming against her ribs. All at once, time compressed. A shadow passed the darkened window. A person was watching her! The red-headed stranger?

Her body moved before her mind. She whirled around, belatedly realizing that the person was reflected in the window, not staring in from the outside. It was a woman, not a man. Jenna pressed a hand to her heart. "Caroline?" she managed, turning around.

"I'm so sorry." Caroine looked apologetic. "You okay? I didn't mean to startle you."

Her mind had been a thousand miles away. Now it was racing. When had Caroline arrived at the Kelseys'? And how long had she been standing there? Had she overheard Jenna say she was pregnant with Seth's baby? She still felt breathless. "You scared me."

Wincing, Caroline brushed back a lock of sunstreaked hair from her forehead and gestured across the hallway, back toward her bedroom as if to indicate she'd just come from there. "Sorry, Jenna. Really, I am. The last thing I wanted to do was to startle you."

Jenna's heart slowed. "No big deal," she managed with a weak smile. "Chasing that guy through the town square must have left me shaky. And Seth seemed so convinced that the man was following me, that I guess I'm getting paranoid."

"You didn't look paranoid when you charged into Marge's wielding that mace."

Jenna chuckled at the recollection, gesturing as Caroline edged a step inside the room. "Come on in." She nodded toward where the wedding dress was draped over the chairs. "Move that if you want. Have a seat."

Caroline looked undecided, then she shook her head. "Thanks, but I think I'll go take a long, hot bath."

Jenna frowned. "I thought you were working until closing time."

Caroline laughed sheepishly. "Me, too. I completely misread the schedule. Tonight was only a partial shift. As it turned out, I stayed an extra hour.

Marge needed to run out and do some errands, so I filled in for an hour. You and Seth must have left just after me.'' Her eyes, always watchful, had settled on Jenna's open suitcase. She frowned. ''I take it you're leaving?''

Jenna managed a nod. ''My work at Molly's is about done. We can finish the rest by fax and mail.''

Caroline nodded. ''Well…I really didn't mean to startle you.'' She jerked her head toward the hallway. ''I was in my room, and, to be perfectly honest, it sounded as if a burglar was over here, rooting around in your things. Actually, I figured you and Seth were still out. And since Seth thought someone was following you…''

''You thought someone was in my room?'' Jenna queried, uneasily thinking of the redhead.

Caroline chuckled softly. ''Silly, huh? Tyler isn't exactly a high-crime kind of town.''

Somehow, the other woman's sudden lopsided grin dispelled Jenna's uneasiness. ''No, it's not. I think New York's just made me paranoid.''

''Expecting menace around every corner?''

Jenna nodded. ''Yeah. But it's nice here.'' She smiled ruefully, surprised at her feelings. ''It's the kind of place where people settle down.''

''Then stay another couple of days,'' Caroline ventured.

''Molly just called, telling me she'd like me to stay, too.''

''You really should.''

With shock, Jenna realized Caroline's eyes had

now settled on the prenatal vitamins on the bedside table. Wishing she'd put them away, Jenna tried to act as if she didn't notice the direction of Caroline's gaze, but when Caroline lifted her eyes, it was clear she'd surmised Jenna was pregnant. For the briefest second, Jenna found herself fighting the impulse to tell everything to this complete stranger. It would feel so good to unburden herself. But ever since Seth confessed he'd never considered having children, she'd known she had to leave Tyler with her secret intact. In Tyler, she'd begun to suspect no secret was safe. Not even with someone such as the mysterious, young Caroline Benning who, like Jenna, just seemed to be passing through town.

No, Jenna's keeping her mouth shut and leaving town was the right thing to do. Earlier she'd slid from the booth at Marge's Diner, telling Seth it had been great to spend the evening with him but that she could see herself home. He'd been both perturbed and curious about her change in attitude.

"I figured you'd at least want another hot chocolate," he'd said.

She'd shrugged. "I guess all the excitement wore me out."

"I don't recall excitement ever wearing you out," he'd returned dryly, not buying her excuse and insisting he walk her back to the Kelseys'. Once there, he'd offered a kiss goodnight. As much as Jenna had wanted to feel his mouth on hers, she'd dodged him.

Now she sighed. "I figure I'll check out tonight," she said to Caroline. "I guess I should go down and see what paperwork Johnny Kelsey needs, so I can get a head start in the morning.''

Caroline looked worried. ''You already have a flight? So soon?''

Jenna nodded. ''It leaves pretty early.''

''Well—'' Caroline edged into the hallway ''—it was nice to meet you. I had fun talking to you during dinner. I'm up early, so I'll make a point of seeing you off.''

Jenna smiled. ''That's so nice of you.'' The gesture, like so many things in Tyler, warmed Jenna, and that fool lump she kept fighting lodged in her throat once more. Reverend Sarah Baron's invitation to church flitted through her mind, too. Yes, she could definitely see why Seth had chosen to return home, even after so many years.

And deep down, Jenna wished she wasn't leaving.

''MR. SPENCER?'' one of the teller's called. ''That party's still on the line.''

Tamping down his anger, Seth glanced toward his office. ''They won't identify themselves?''

''No, sir. I'm sorry. Should I tell them you can't take the call otherwise?''

''No. I'll take it.''

Glancing around the lobby of the bank, Seth blew out a soft, murderous sigh. Since when had his life become such a living hell? The front doors had only opened ten minutes ago, and already everything seemed to be going wrong.

But no, he thought angrily.

Actually, things had upended and headed south before he'd even left home this morning. He'd scorched his shirt while ironing it, leaving a blackened-yellow streak near the armpit, then he'd spilled coffee down a tie Jenna had gotten him last Christmas. Even worse, since he was still in New York mode, he'd forgotten he wasn't going to pass any shoe-shine stands on his way to work, which meant his oxfords were caked with mud. He'd just exited the men's room, where he'd attacked the shoes with a paper towel, hoping to do damage control.

Somebody had the nerve to snigger. "Trouble getting dressed, Mr. Spencer?"

Another teller giggled. "Need a woman, Mr. Spencer?"

"Probably."

And not just any woman, he thought, taking long strides toward his office. He needed Jenna. He'd awakened this morning, feeling sorely tempted to charge right over to the Kelsey Boarding House and demand to know what had happened last night. In the park, he'd been so sure things were going well. He'd opened up to her more than he ever had. He was loathe to admit it, of course, but since last seeing Jenna, he had read a book called *What Women Want*. He'd done exactly what it said. He'd made himself vulnerable by talking about his mother, hadn't he? Hadn't Jenna understood he was trying to get to know her better, despite the fact that she was marrying someone else?

And then, at Marge's Diner, while Jenna was all

but making fun of him for wanting to keep her safe, he'd shared his doubts about getting married. He'd admitted romance hadn't worked out for him any more than it had for Quinn. He'd confessed that he'd been so unsure of himself in relationships that he'd never even really considered having kids. He'd stared at her intently when he'd said that. Surely she'd felt the words, right?

Dammit, he hadn't wanted or expected Jenna's sympathy. But shouldn't she have been touched by his efforts? Shouldn't she have been impressed by his honesty? He'd wanted her to know that he was taking full responsibility for whatever hadn't worked out in their relationship. Whatever happened in their relationship was *his* fault, not hers. He shook his head. Never in his life would he understand women.

"And she's marrying Dom, anyway," he muttered.

Stopping at the threshold of his office, he could only glare at the desk. He barely even noticed the blinking red light on the phone. Instead, he was seeing Jenna lying on the desk, her legs bare, her skirt thrust up above her waist, her rose-colored skin glowing with the same reflective light as the shiny mahogany surface.

Suddenly, he wished she would get married. And soon, too. Maybe that would get her out of his mind. With a start, he headed toward the desk again. Feeling more foul-tempered than he ever had during a bad day on Wall Street, he didn't bother to lift the receiver, but only punched speaker phone and the waiting extension. His tone turned all-business.

''Seth Spencer here.'' When a raspy sound emanated from the speaker, he squinted. ''Hello? Can you please speak up? I can't hear you.''

''Seth Spencer?''

At least he *thought* the person had said his name. Whoever it was—he couldn't tell if the caller was male or female—sounded like a killer from an old B movie, though. Low and hoarse, this was the kind of voice that generally wound up demanding money. In a flash, Seth considered that the bank was about to be robbed, then he came to his senses and said, ''I can barely hear you. Sorry. I think we may have a bad connection. Hold on and let me take you off Speaker phone.'' Lifting the receiver from the cradle, he spoke directly into the mouthpiece. ''There. Is that any better?''

It wasn't. ''This is Seth Spencer?''

Yeah. And is this a hired gun? he wanted to say, his frown deepening. There was something familiar here, not in the voice itself but in the cadences. Seth could swear he'd heard it before—not often, maybe only once or twice. Of course, that could be his imagination. ''Yes,'' he said calmly. ''This is Seth Spencer.'' He sat down slowly and deliberately then, reaching for a pad of paper, knowing something was wrong.

''We need to talk.''

Seth could barely make out the words. What did this person want? Money? He tightened his grip around the phone. ''Talk?'' he echoed, buying time to find a pen. ''About?''

"Jenna Robinson. I have some information."

Fear flushed through his veins like ice, then brief denial. He tried to tell himself that the person hadn't really said Jenna's name. "Who is this?" he demanded, his senses on alert.

"I can't tell you who I am."

The hell you can't, he wanted to growl, but he knew he couldn't afford to antagonize the caller. He swallowed hard. "This is about Jenna?" he forced himself to continue, his mind racing. *The redheaded man,* he realized. *That's who it is.* Everything fell into place. Maybe the man was someone he'd met on Wall Street, at Goldman Sachs. Maybe he'd followed Jenna from New York, knowing her and Seth's history, and he'd kidnapped her. Now he was going to ask for money from the S&L.

Seth cut his eyes toward the vault thinking, *You can have anything.* Not that he'd announce that to the other party on the line. Cursing silently, he wished the bank had better security. "Jenna," he managed. "Can you assure me she's safe? Is she there? Can you put her on the line?"

A gasp sounded. Seth frowned. Obviously, this was no professional. In fact, it now sounded as if an old-fashioned doily was being held over the mouthpiece to disguise the voice. The voice said, "I didn't mean to imply something happened to her."

Relief flooded him. "She's all right?"

"Of course," announced the voice. "She's fine. But she's pregnant. You're going to be a daddy."

Chapter Seven

Pregnant. The word was still ringing in Seth's ears an hour later as he tugged Jenna toward the parking lot.

"Be careful! I'm going to drop Gretchen!"

She wasn't. "I trust you to hang on to her," muttered Seth.

As if to prove he was right, Gretchen giggled. "Seth!" Jenna bit out between clenched teeth. "People are staring!"

"Every unmarried man in the Madison airport, anyway," Seth agreed. He was gripping Jenna's elbow with one hand and, with the other, pushing a dolly stacked with her suitcases and the damnable wedding dress, and now he stilled his steps just long enough to send her a long, level, assessing look. Wind was tossing glorious, silken-brown, red-streaked feathered hair across her cheeks and even now, despite the circumstances, Seth felt utterly compelled to touch it. Almost against his will, he took in the delicate, transparent white blouse she was wearing under her leather coat, and when his eyes drifted, they settled where the fluted collar fluttered against bare skin, stroking her long, creamy neck and the decorative henna scroll work encircling it. He knew better than to torture himself by letting his eyes drop, but they did anyway, lingering on Jenna's endless, slender, dancer's legs, which were encased in red fishnets.

He shook his head as his gaze returned to hers, meeting dark, round, wire-rimmed sunglasses. What was he going to do with this woman? Somehow, despite her outfit, she looked so maternal holding Gretchen that Seth could barely move. For a second he actually quit breathing. Wide bands seemed to circle his chest and constrict, squeezing every last bit of air from his lungs. Without her even knowing it, this woman was bringing him to his knees. Maybe she'd done so the very first time he'd ever seen her in the art gallery.

Coming to his senses, he yanked her elbow. Her high-heeled, witch-style, black demi-boots skittered across the concrete as he continued manhandling her toward his Blazer, holding her elbow even more firmly now than he had when he found her returning the Cadillac at the rent-a-wreck desk.

"One of those guys might decide to come to my rescue, you know," Jenna muttered indignantly, dropping a light, absent kiss onto Gretchen's forehead before righteously jerking her head toward the sidewalk.

Glancing around, Seth noted a few tall, rangy cowboys in dusty jeans and scuffed boots who were, indeed, lounging near the airport doorway. They sized Seth up, their eyes lingering where he kept a proprietorial grip on Jenna. They weren't the type of men who took kindly to rich men in fancy, tailored suits getting the girl. "Judging from the looks of some of those guys, you're probably safer with me." Seth missed a beat. "And given my mood, that's saying something, Jenna."

"If you intend for me to go back to Tyler," she returned haughtily as if trying to hold on to some last semblance of dignity, "I'll at least need my car, won't I?"

He rolled his eyes. "I think Tyler, Wisconsin, can do without that Cadillac."

Her chin rose a notch. "I liked that car," she defended. "What was wrong with it?"

"Everything. By now, the quilters at Worthington House are probably circulating a city petition to keep it off the street."

"The minister's husband said he'd fix it."

"Give it a rest, Jenna."

"I will when you let me and Gretchen go."

He wasn't about to, even though nothing more than Jenna's hushed, husky voice was threatening to unhinge him. No way was she leaving Wisconsin. Was Jenna crazy? Were pregnant women even allowed to fly in airplanes? He could swear he'd heard they weren't supposed to. He shot Jenna a sideways glance, his eyes settling in the proximity of her belly. She didn't look pregnant yet, but he'd stayed on the phone with the mysterious caller long enough to find out it was his baby. Not Dom's. *His.*

Seth's mouth went dry. He was going to be a father. The second he'd heard, a vision of the new house on Maple Street had flashed through his mind, and his first coherent thought was that he'd fortunately bought exactly the kind of family place he and Jenna would need. Then he'd recalled she'd never intended to tell him about the pregnancy, and that she was marrying Dom. With his free hand, Seth somehow finished pushing the dolly to the curb, opened the side door of the Blazer, then tossed her bags inside. Dammit, did she really think Seth was going to let another man raise his baby without a fight?

When he turned around, she was still staring at him. "I'm sorry I didn't tell you I was leaving town, Seth. I should have. It was rude of me."

So that's why she thought he was mad? She was clutching Gretchen, who was staring curiously at Seth as if she'd never even seen him before. She'd definitely never seen him this mad. Hating the fact that the poor kid was witnessing all this tension, he said, "Just give me the car seat, Jenna."

"Seth!" Jenna gaped at him as he took it from her, then she shifted Gretchen from one hip to the other. "I was late and they already made a boarding call. My plane's about to leave."

"Without you," he assured. Vaguely, he felt relieved. Deep down, he knew if Jenna had really wanted to take that flight, she would have, but she'd decided to come with him instead. She didn't like feeling manhandled, though, so she wasn't coming without a fight. Climbing inside the sport-utility, he attached the car seat, then gestured for Jenna to hand over the baby, "Here. Let me have her."

When Jenna didn't bother to move, Seth could only guess at what was going on in her mind. "You can't come to the airport and get me like this," she complained as he wiggled Gretchen from her embrace, offered the baby a smacking kiss of assurance that made her giggle, then strapped her into her seat. Jenna said, "Seth, what's this really about?"

"As if you don't know."

He was pleased to hear her voice shake with sudden uncertainty. "What's that supposed to mean?"

His mouth set grimly as he opened the passenger-side door for her. "You know exactly what it means. Get in."

Let her sweat. He couldn't help but feel a rush of pleasure at her guilty expression. Yes, if he'd been looking for proof of the information she'd withheld from him, it was completely evident now. Her cheeks were flushed a deep rose color, and beneath the smooth, kissable surface of her delectable neck, the pulse was beating wildly out of control. "I said I'm sorry for not telling you good-bye," she suddenly said miserably, and then she climbed inside and simply slammed the door.

Circling to his side of the car, he got in and pulled from the curb, glancing in the rearview mirror to make sure Gretchen was well-situated. The little sweetheart waved at him. Lifting a hand from the steering wheel, he waved back. Not that his mood improved. In fact, his fury spiked again when, as he pulled off the ramp to the highway, Jenna leaned forward and flicked on the radio.

On impulse, he flicked it off.

Her voice was terse. "You have a problem with the radio?"

Yeah, he wanted to say. *It's mine. Just the way the baby you're carrying is mine.*

All at once, he wanted to come at her shouting. But then, he'd worked in the financial industry long enough to learn how to hold his temper. Yes, in the world of high finance, a man learned to pick his moments. He just wished dealing with Jenna was as easy as mulling over stock tips. Once they were on the highway, he told himself to wait until they were in Tyler before they talked. It was better not to argue while he was driving, and yet anger and curiosity were eating him alive. Feeling torn, he glanced from the windshield to her face. "C'mon, Jen. Don't you have something to say to me?"

Removing her sunglasses, she stared at him a long moment, those bright green slivers of eyes looking cool and watchful. "What did you hear? Why did you really come to the airport like this? And don't play coy," she said. "I know it's not just because you want to see me, Seth."

"Dammit, Jenna," he suddenly returned in a soft, exasperated growl, his temper finally getting the best of him, "are you pregnant?" He cut his eyes toward her again, his heart nearly stopping since the pause in conversation seemed to go on forever. Staring at her, he suddenly felt like a fool. What if he was wrong? "You *are* pregnant, right?"

Or was she?

He sent a surreptitious glance toward her belly, but she was wearing a coat. She hadn't *felt* pregnant when they'd made love on his desk, either. What if the call he'd gotten at the bank was a crank? What if it had been one of his brothers, jerking his chain?

When she finally spoke, Jenna's voice was so soft he could have floated on it. "Yes." He heard a catch in her throat. "I'm sorry, Seth."

Sorry? What was she talking about? Relief flooded him, and only then did he realize how badly he wanted this. His eyes sought and found hers. "Sorry?"

She was fiddling with her hands, clasping and unclasping them in her lap. "Did Dom call you?"

Despite his elation, Seth blew out an angry sigh. He hardly wanted to feel indebted to his adversary for making sure he got this information. "I really don't know who called," he said honestly, trying to keep his emotions in check since he and Jenna were obviously going to have to work out some kind of lasting relationship, if only for the baby's sake. "They wouldn't identify themselves. Actually," he added, still wanting to deny that he owed Dom anything, "I think it was a woman."

"Oh, God," Jenna murmured. "Maybe it was Caroline Benning. Last night, she came into my room when I was packing, and she saw some prenatal vitamins. Maybe she overheard me talking to Dom...."

"Dom," Seth couldn't help but mutter, training his narrowing eyes through the windshield.

He could feel Jenna's gaze, hot and intense on his face. "What's wrong with Dom? You always liked him."

"Jenna—" Seth bit out the words before he could stop himself. "Right now, I'd like nothing more than to erase his name from the Book of Life, okay?"

He thought she sounded hopeful. "You would?"

Hell yes, he would. Seth forced himself to exhale slowly. "I understand that you've apparently fallen in love with the guy, I do. But were you really going to leave Tyler without telling me about this baby? Were you really going to let my child call another man 'Daddy'?" As he spoke the words, another wave of disbelief washed over him. "We may not have shared our darkest secrets, but I thought I knew you, Jenna. We've spent a lot of time together." When he glanced at her, he was utterly stunned to see the righteous tilt of her chin.

"You do know me," she countered. "But after what you said last night, any woman would have left town. It was the only right thing for me to do."

He shifted his weight in the seat, glancing briefly through the windshield before his eyes sought hers. When their gazes meshed, an unexpected jolt of awareness went through him. Was he really going to have a baby by this woman? His mind still couldn't quite process it. "After what I said?"

She stared at him, slack-jawed. "Seth, last night in Marge's Diner, you said you'd never considered marrying. You said that when it came to kids, you felt exactly *like* your brother, Quinn.''

Seth uttered a curse under his breath. ''I said I'd never considered having kids,'' he growled. ''I didn't say I didn't like them.''

Jenna's voice sounded oddly small. ''Oh.''

''Jenna,'' he continued, sure he'd never felt this exasperated in his life. ''I was trying to talk to you last night, to open up. I wanted you to know you weren't responsible for any failure in our relationship.'' Pausing, he shook his head in consternation, wishing she didn't do such dangerous things to the blood whirling through his insides. ''How could you take a freelance job in my hometown—a job I hooked you up with, by the way—and come here to work for Molly Blake, never intending to tell me you were pregnant? What kind of person would do that? Did you know before I left New York?''

She shook her head, looking miserable. ''After.''

That gave him pause. He could see her point of view now. Clearly, she'd felt he walked out on her, not making plans to keep in touch, and when she found out about the baby, she'd been hesitant to contact him. He hardened himself, not feeling particularly inclined to give her the benefit of the doubt. ''How long have you been seeing Dom?''

''He proposed when he found out about the baby.''

Why? To give Seth's son or daughter a name? This was really too much. Not that Seth could ask more about the nature of Dom's intentions. Every time he tried to bring up Jenna and Dom's relationship, she exploded. She seemed to think Seth's curiosity indicated disbelief about her marriage potential, as if she were somehow, intrinsically, unlovable. Inwardly, he cursed her folks. He'd never met them, and while they sounded superficially nice enough, they hadn't loved Jenna the way she'd needed. Seth's mother had abandoned him, but Jenna's trust level was even lower than his. "Jenna," he forced himself to plunge on, trying another tack, "if you'd gone back to New York, I could have lived a lifetime not knowing I had a child. Do you realize what you've done? Do you understand the implications of that?"

"I would have told you," she recanted. "Eventually." Her voice broke, and for the briefest second, he was sure the indomitable Jenna was dangerously close to tears. "I really thought you meant what you said last night, Seth. Honestly, I thought you'd be ugly about me having a baby."

His heart missed a beat. How could she be so off the mark about what he felt? Were her assumptions about him the problem? Or was he really that bad at communicating his emotions? "No, Jenna, I'm glad."

Her words hitched. "You are?"

"Yes." But she'd never be convinced. "I'm mad, though. You weren't going to tell me. The day you came to the bank, you said Dom insisted you tell me about the marriage, but it was the baby he wanted me to know about, wasn't it?"

She nodded, and as she swallowed, he could see her throat working. Then she said the very last thing he expected. ''Seth, do you remember that redheaded guy in the white car?''

Seth nodded.

''Well, I hate to cut all this short, but I think he's following us.''

''EVER SINCE SHE arrived here from New York, that man's been following her,'' Seth assured coolly, his voice calm, controlled and more lethal than Jenna had ever heard it.

Inside the Tyler police substation, a tall, thin, thirty-something man whose nameplate identified him as Stew Cary patted a black uniform pocket, looking for a pen. ''I'll take a report, if you really think it's necessary, Mr. Spencer.''

''Oh, I think it's necessary,'' said Seth.

Shifting Gretchen from one hip to the other and ignoring that her back was aching from carrying her so long, Jenna took a deep breath and held it for an anxious moment before exhaling. ''You know,'' she put in, ''we've been trying to file a report since last night.''

''That so?'' inquired the officer.

''Yes,'' she managed. ''That's so.'' So why didn't the police seem more interested? In a town as seemingly uneventful as Tyler, she'd expected the local lawmen to be happy for a crime to solve. Despite her indignation, Jenna was also half-glad the man in the white car had reentered her life. At least Stew Cary, not she, was now the target for Seth's slow-burning fury. Not that Jenna was feeling particularly patient with the officer. "Mr. Spencer—er, I mean Seth—saw this man outside Molly Blake's house the other day," she continued, feeling for the first time since her arrival in Tyler that she and Seth had become a team again. "Molly Blake is—"

"I know who Molly Blake is," assured Stew pleasantly.

As near as Jenna could tell everybody in Tyler was acquainted. "Well, then, have you noticed that bunch of trees just across the street from her house?" Before Stew could respond, Jenna plunged ahead, suddenly feeling panicked and secretly hoping the redheaded stranger wasn't really intentionally following her. "Yesterday, during a meeting with Seth, I was parked under those trees. When I pulled away from the curb, he said a redheaded man with a handlebar mustache followed me. It might be a coincidence, but—"

"It's no coincidence," Seth cut in.

"The man *was* parked right behind me," Jenna admitted. "And he might have been waiting for me to leave Molly's." Her heart missed a fearful beat and, to calm herself, she dropped a quick kiss on Gretchen's head. "I mean, I didn't think anything about it at the time, but..."

Seth nodded. "He was watching for her. Definitely. And he was driving the same car today. It's a white compact."

"A Neon," confirmed Jenna. "I recognize them. My friend Sue drives one."

Seth's mouth set grimly. "Unfortunately, we didn't get the license plate numbers."

"If Gretchen hadn't been with us," Jenna reminded firmly, "we would have, Seth." He was being too hard on himself. After Jenna had alerted Seth to the white car—she'd seen it in her side view mirror—he'd taken the next exit from the highway. Sure enough, the white car had followed. Pretending to pull into a gas station, Seth quickly circled the pumps and gave chase, but out of concern for Gretchen, he stopped, letting the man go.

"We could have caught him in the Blazer," Seth muttered.

True. But Gretchen's wails had served as reminder of the potential danger, and Seth hadn't wanted to exceed the speed limit with the baby in the car. Just thinking of his protective nature made Jenna's heart squeeze tightly. Why did Seth have to be so sweet sometimes? The kind of man to whom she'd entrust her life? And why hadn't she ever understood how difficult it was for him to talk about his emotions?

Or am I being too easy on him again?

Didn't she deserve love, trust and protection to come to her more easily? Was she going to wind up fighting for affection again, the way she felt she had with her parents? Wasn't she forgetting that she'd brought her worn copy of *Women Who Love Too Much* to Tyler for good reason?

For a second, Jenna was a million miles away. Bright rays of sunlight were streaming through the streaked substation window, and now they heightened, blurred and mixed, until she realized the trouble wasn't the light, but her vision. Watery tears had sprung to her eyes. Had she heard Seth correctly? she wondered now. Before they saw the redheaded stranger, was Seth really saying he wanted to be a daddy?

Her arm tightened around Gretchen's waist and she pulled the baby closer, reminding herself that she needed to call Dom soon, otherwise he'd be expecting their flight to arrive. She still didn't even know if Sue had come home yet. And what was Jenna going to do about her relationship with Dom? Or with Seth? Pushing aside her doubts, she tried not to wonder. She could definitely use a brief mental vacation from her anxieties at the moment. Yesterday, she'd thought she could marry a man she didn't love passionately. But what about now? Now that Seth had said he wanted their coming baby, weren't things different?

Shaking her head to clear it of confusion, she eyed Stew Cary. Not that the cop had bothered to move. He was merely chewing the inside of his cheek thoughtfully, his friendly, sparkling blue eyes making him look about as lethal as Daffy Duck. When it came to being served and protected, Jenna would rather ride shotgun with Seth Spencer any day. Lanky and agile with light blond hair, Stew Cary looked like Jimmy Stewart, but he was obviously nowhere near as competent as the heroic characters that actor had played. "So, you really think this guy's following her?" Stew asked now, addressing Seth rather than Jenna as he seated himself in an office chair, then rolled in front of a desk.

"*I* think he's following me," Jenna returned, hating the implication that Seth could speak for her.

Seemingly ignoring her, Stew opened a drawer and scrounged around inside it. "Sorry. I can't seem to find the citizen complaint forms."

Jenna winced. Judging from the murderous way Seth was now looking at the officer, he might soon need something far more substantial—like a stack of death certificates. "Can't we just use some regular paper?" Jenna suggested. "It's only a statement. We just want something on record, should we have any more trouble."

Stew shook his head. "Nope. Need the forms. You know how particular the U.S. government is."

Not nearly as particular as Seth Spencer, she thought. Seth was wearing a suit so perfectly tailored that seeing him in it made Jenna's mouth water, and now he shoved his hands deeply into the trouser pockets as if half afraid he might inadvertently reach out and strangle the other man. "Shush," Jenna murmured to Gretchen, gently removing the baby's hand when it reached for one of Jenna's dangle earrings. "We'll be out of here in no time, sweetheart."

"We're not leaving until we get to the bottom of this," Seth assured, his eyes riveted on Stew, who was now pulling a stack of yellow forms from the drawer.

"I guess we can use these," murmured Stew. "Basically, you just want to make a statement, right?"

Seth shut his eyes and Jenna assumed he was counting to ten. "That's what we said."

Jenna hardly wanted to fan the flames, but she was starting to feel as exasperated as Seth looked. "I'm not sure I understand why you're having so much trouble with our doing so. Seth saw a man follow me from Molly Blake's house. Then, last night, we think the same man was spying on us in the town square. We chased him toward Marge's Diner."

Stew glanced up from a yellow form. "Couldn't he have been out walking?"

Jenna glanced at Seth. He was towering over the other man, staring down coldly at him, and now a tiny muscle inside Seth's cheek was starting to quiver dangerously. "I guess he *was* out walking," said Seth, faint sarcasm curling through the words, "right up until he started running." He paused. "Because I was chasing him."

"And just now he followed us from the airport," Jenna added.

Seth shot her a quick glance, then said, "Look, Officer, I know most people in Tyler, but I don't know you—"

Stew Cary grinned and thrust out his hand as if Seth and Jenna were newcomers at a church social, instead of potential crime victims looking for help inside a police station. "Stew Cary," he said. "I'm new to town. Actually, I think I'm going to be working for Brick Bauer over at the Benton substation, but Coop said I should come in and learn some of the ropes."

Seth didn't bother to shake the extended hand.

It took everything she had, but Jenna held her

tongue. To her, it didn't even look as if Stew Cary was working. Judging from the empty coffee cups and doughnut boxes in the room, not to mention Stew's confusion over the appropriate complaint forms, he should probably be seeking another kind of employment.

Seth blew out an audible sigh. "Maybe we should come back. When will Cooper Night Hawk be in the office?"

Stew shrugged. "Hard to tell. He's been caught up with some felon who's been robbing convenience stores upstate."

"That's what we were told last night, when we called from the diner," Jenna said, trying not to worry. It was dawning on her that if the man was following her, the Tyler police wouldn't offer much protection.

Stew glanced at her, now lifting a form from the stack and clicking the top of a ballpoint pen. "Now," he began, "you two folks say the man had red hair?"

"And a handlebar mustache," growled Seth.

How many times did they need to repeat themselves? "We'll give you three guesses as to what color the car was," Jenna couldn't help but challenge.

Stew Cary didn't look the least bit perturbed. "White," he said, writing. "I got that much. Now, you said he had a handlebar mustache? Do you mean like the ones the stagecoach robbers always have on old Wild West movies?"

Sighing, Jenna suddenly caught a faint whiff of the fact that Gretchen had dirtied a diaper. Noting the slow downturn of the baby's usually smiling mouth, Jenna exchanged a long glance with Seth. "Maybe we should just come back," she murmured, hardly caring if the officer overheard.

Seth looked undecided. Withdrawing his hands from his trouser pockets, he placed them on his hips, then he lifted his gaze from Stew Cary. Slowly, Seth's eyes panned the room, taking in the empty foam cups and doughnut boxes. "You've been extremely helpful, Officer Cary," he finally deadpanned, "but I think we'd better call Cooper Night Hawk at home."

A moment later, right before the door to the substation closed behind them, Jenna heard Stew Cary call out, "Glad you felt I was helpful. We do aim to please. Guys like me never forget that it's the public paying our salaries."

Chapter Eight

Jenna was peering through the windshield, and as she unbuttoned her coat, Seth did his level best not to notice how the seat belt was straining between her breasts, accentuating the full mounds about which he'd been dreaming ever since her arrival in Tyler. The hemline of her already short skirt had risen, too, and red fishnets, Seth silently decided, could be the world's first real cure for erectile dysfunction. Not that he was having any such trouble himself.

Craning her head, Jenna firmly pushed her slipping sunglasses back onto the bridge of her nose and stared at an intersection he'd just passed. "Isn't the Kelsey Boarding House that way? Didn't you miss a turn, Seth?"

The woman was definitely getting to know her way around Tyler. "You could be a native," he remarked, wishing she was, especially with the baby coming. Somehow, all this seemed so crazy. How could he let Jenna go back to New York? How could they work things out when they lived a thousand miles apart? How could he stand living so far from his own child?

He started to bring up the concerns that were on the tip of his tongue, then decided they'd have to wait, at least until he and Jenna reached his house. They needed to sit down and really talk things through. "I don't think that's the best place for you and Gretchen right now, not with this guy following you, Jen."

"I'll be fine."

"You don't know that," Seth said decisively, spinning the steering wheel and rounding another corner, still fighting his temper over the way Stew Cary had treated them just now. Under ordinary circumstances, Seth would protect Jenna with his life, but given her pregnancy, he felt even more vigilant. "Can you believe what passes for police protection in Tyler?" he continued with a grimace. "As soon as we get to my place, we'll call Cooper Night Hawk. It's too bad he wasn't at the substation. He's a good cop. Once he hears what's going on, he'll help us out." Seth still couldn't fathom why Stew Cary hadn't been more concerned about Jenna's safety. "I just wish we'd caught the guy last night."

Jenna barely seemed to have registered Seth's tirade. She sounded faint. "Did you say your place?"

He nodded, running a hand worriedly through his dark hair and still thinking of Stew. "With cops like that around, it's a good thing Tyler's not exactly Crime Central. Do you need me to stop for anything? Food? Soda?"

Jenna groaned. "Diapers. I was just about to get some at the airport," she added, shooting him a pointed glance. "And I need to call Sue. She'll be upset about Gretchen not coming home today."

Ignoring Jenna's pique, Seth lifted his gaze to the rearview mirror, a smile tilting the corner of his mouth as he looked at Gretchen who sensed his attention and giggled. "It's nice to be able to see her for an extra day."

"What?" Jenna returned, the slightest hint of teasing infusing her words. "Do you intend to let us leave someday?"

Seth chuckled softly. "You don't want to be my hostage?" When Jenna didn't immediately answer, he glanced again at Gretchen and said, "I think we can swing by the store. She doesn't look too fussy yet."

"Fussy or not, we need diapers."

"Hey, kid," he added, still grinning at the baby and wondering if he and Jenna would have a boy or a girl. *I want both.* The unexpected thought blindsided him, stealing his smile and touching him somewhere so deep inside that it almost hurt. How, in only a few days, could he have gone from never considering having kids to wanting two? Seth wasn't sure, but since he'd grown up with brothers, he couldn't imagine being an only child as Jenna had been. But was he really ready to start a family? Was he interested in dissuading Jenna from marrying Dom, so that he could marry her himself? Could he let go of the past enough to do so? Could any man really ever get over something so mind-boggling as being abandoned by his own mother?

Seth chewed his lip. To someone who'd never experienced what he had the day his mother left, his confusion would seem ludicrous. Even now, it seemed that way to him. How could he be such a highly functioning adult, and still have the angry teenager living inside him? He didn't so much mind that Violet had left town—in this day and age, people often divorced—but she'd never written or called. It was as if her sons had never even existed. Hadn't she loved them at all?

Ever since Jenna's arrival in Tyler, Seth's emotional reality was becoming clearer to him. It was as if, without ever understanding it, he'd lived with a veil hanging over his life that had now been whisked away. The day his mother left town he'd gotten the message, loud and clear, that he wasn't worthy of a woman's love. When the woman he'd loved chose to give her heart to another man, Seth had decided never to love again. Crazy, he thought now, that something so long ago had stopped him from living to the fullest. Like a fool, he'd let those crippling past emotions remain alive inside him, festering and unresolved, instead of pursuing Jenna.

For a second, he hated Dom. No doubt, Dom possessed a past history—everybody did—but Dom had dealt with his, which had allowed him to propose to Jenna and offer to father Seth's child. Looking back at the time he'd spent in New York with Jenna, Seth could pinpoint the exact times when he'd gotten scared. Over and over, as Jenna got too close, fear that felt akin to terror would set in, way deep down, gnawing at his insides. He'd denied it, too. Fear of loving a female wasn't exactly the kind of emotion to which an adult man enjoyed admitting.

Still, without ever fully acknowledging it, Seth had distanced himself from Jenna. Sometimes, he wouldn't call for a while. Or midweekend he'd suddenly feel antsy about spending so much time with her, and he'd make up excuses so he could head back to his own apartment. Now sadness washed over him. For a smart guy, he could be awfully dumb. Why hadn't he noticed how much of his unresolved past had remained operative in his present life?

Jenna's voice cut into his reverie. "Look, Seth, I know you're worried about that guy, but I don't know if our staying together is a good idea…"

He shook his head in protest, hating that she didn't want to spend the night with him. "Afraid Dom'll get jealous?"

She stiffened. "Can we leave Dom out of this?"

"Sure." For now. But he wasn't taking her back to the boarding house when she was being followed. "Sorry, Jenna," he finally continued, "but for safety's sake, you and Gretchen should come home with me. Besides, we need to talk." Feeling suddenly breathless, he added, "About the baby."

She swallowed hard. "True."

When he glanced toward her again, the silent protest remaining in her eyes shot through him as painfully as a bullet. He thought he noticed other things in her expression, too—desire and anticipation—but that didn't much improve his flagging mood. Only two months ago she'd always been thrilled to see him.

His lips set in a grim line. "You make it seem as if coming to my house is a fate worse than death," he couldn't help but remark. "Last night I thought you said you liked it."

She was anxiously fiddling with the handle to the glove box. "Your house is…" She paused as if trying to find a suitable word, then settled on "wonderful."

"And so?"

Her previous pique returned. "Whether I like it or not isn't the point."

He raised a dark eyebrow. "And what is?"

Looking thoroughly unsettled, she turned toward him, now wiggling out of her leather coat as if she had too much nervous energy and needed to occupy herself. "Seth, Gretchen and I are supposed to be on a plane right now, headed back to New York."

Headed back to Dom. It simply wasn't in Seth Spencer to allow that right now. "Don't worry, Jenna," he said dryly, "it's not as if I'm going to attack you."

"Oh, please!" she burst out, draping her coat pointedly over her lap. "You're so dramatic."

"There are four bedrooms in the house," he assured, ploughing on in a voice that was gruffer than he'd intended. "You can have mine. It's got a lock if you feel you need it." Not that he wouldn't gladly kick down the door if he had a mind to.

She was eyeing him warily. "Sorry," she murmured. "I didn't mean to ruffle your feathers."

Somehow, he managed to keep his voice calm. "As many times as we've spent the night together, I really don't think coming to my house should be such a big deal for you."

Blowing out a peeved sigh, she said, "You make me sound like a complete prude, and you know better. I'm just protesting because…"

Because you still want me, too? He fought not to say the words. Already, he'd been open enough about his feelings—and without reciprocation. If Jenna still had feelings for him, she'd have to announce that on her own. "Because?"

Her expression faintly stricken, she stared through the windshield. "Oh, I don't know," she said with another quick sigh. "I don't want to talk about this right now. Let's just go to the store, okay?"

Glancing her way again, he could see countless unasked questions haunting those heart-stopping green eyes. They seemed to be asking if he really had more on his mind than playing bodyguard and protecting her and Gretchen from the man in the white car. He was sorely tempted to assure her he'd kill to have her in his bed tonight, but then she might change her mind and insist on going to the Kelseys'. "You really can't expect me to leave you alone tonight," he finally persuaded, his voice lowering and becoming tinged with seduction. "Not with a maniac on the loose."

"I wouldn't be alone. I'd be with a whole clan of Kelseys," she reminded pertly, catching her emotional balance. "And now you're calling the guy a maniac. Earlier, he was just a redheaded stranger."

Seth couldn't help the smile that flickered over his

lips. He was more worried about Jenna than he wanted to let on, but she was right. The closer she got to his house and his bed, the more dangerous Seth was making the man out to be. He shrugged. ''I changed my mind. The man's a menace, and you need protection.''

''To be perfectly honest, you're scaring me, Seth.'' She sent him a long, assessing, sideways glance. ''I think you're blowing this whole thing out of proportion.''

''I hope so,'' he said honestly.

Now she looked worried. ''You really think I'm in some sort of danger?''

He chewed thoughtfully on his lip and considered what to tell her as he pulled in front of the store. Sighing and glancing back in the direction of his house, he tried not to admit how nervous he actually felt about having Jenna under his roof. Given how many times they'd slept together, it seemed strange that he was worried about being alone with her. But that was precisely the point. Usually he and Jenna had what could only be described as sex fests. What would they do now, tonight, alone in a house with a baby, and without sex on the agenda?

Well, he wasn't going to try to seduce her tonight, despite how much he wanted her. *She's not yours, anyway, Seth,* said a voice. *No woman's a possession, and Jenna says she's marrying Dom. Why can't you respect that? Hell, if you had any class, you'd have let her go before now.*

Turning off the Blazer's engine, Seth licked at lips

that had gone dry. Wishing he wasn't so conflicted about her, he shot her a surreptitious glance. Damn if he didn't want to flay her verbally for not telling him about the baby, but he wanted to hold her close, too. With sudden quiet, burning desperation, he imagined himself molding his hands over her belly as they talked about the baby. He could see himself stroking and tasting her skin as he tongued her navel. What a fool he'd been! What kind of man would take making love to Jenna Robinson for granted?

On a flash of insight, Seth was sure he'd look back on his life years from now only to find that the tumble on his desk with Jenna was nothing more than their last hurrah. By then they'd be sharing some sort of joint custody, and she'd be having more children with Dom.

Sighing, he glanced toward the store. "You want to wait here while I run in?"

She shot him a droll glance. "Are you sure the man in the white car won't attack me?"

"Life's full of surprises, so watch out," he shot back, then he watched as she reached into the back, scrounging in the seat for a rattle Gretchen had dropped.

As she resettled herself in the passenger seat, she said, "I really think it might be better if I went back to the boarding house, don't you?"

"No, I really am worried about this guy." Rifling a hand through his hair, he wondered if he should say more. He didn't want to scare Jenna, and yet he needed to voice his concerns.

She took off her sunglasses as if to get a better look at him, but only wound up squinting his way, probably against the strong sun shining through the windshield. "What's wrong? I feel like there's something you're not telling me."

"Earlier, when I got that call at the bank," he admitted, "a number of things went through my mind, and while I don't want to worry you…"

Her eyes narrowed, and her lips started to curl downward into a decidedly sexy pout. "For someone not wanting to worry me, you're starting to do a good job."

"I want you to be on the lookout, Jen. You've got to stay alert in case something happens."

She was trying not to look alarmed. "C'mon, Seth. Nothing's going to happen."

She was talking about the stranger, but suddenly Seth was thinking about tonight. She desired him. He'd felt it last night when he'd kissed her in the street. The touch of their lips had been fleeting, but pure, raging heat had coursed through him, pooling in his belly and making his groin tug with insufferable arousal. She'd responded, too, just as surely as she had on his desk. Maybe she thought Dom would make a better husband, but Seth was no fool. The more the shock about her upcoming nuptials wore off, the more objectively Seth could recall how Dom and Jenna interacted. God knew, Seth had seen them together often enough, since they were all good friends, but even the most casual observer would know that Dom and Jenna shared no real sparks. Of course, Jenna might marry Dom anyway. So far, that sure seemed to be her intention.

"I really don't want to worry you, Jenna," Seth continued now, completing his earlier thought, "but when I got the call at the bank, a number of things went through my mind."

"Such as?"

Seth shrugged. "Maybe that guy knew us from New York."

Her eyes widened as if that was the last thing she'd expected him to say. "What makes you think that?"

"I don't know. Look, are you positive you haven't seen him before?"

Anxiously, silently, Jenna twisted her diamond engagement ring until Seth had to fight not to reach across the seat and simply remove it from her finger. She shook her head. "I didn't get a good look at him, but I don't think I've ever met anyone who meets his description."

"Not in the gallery?"

Jenna shook her head.

"What about when you were in art school?"

"Nope."

"Well, I might have met him on Wall Street."

"Wall Street?"

"Yeah. Maybe it's somebody I worked with."

"Maybe? Wouldn't you have remembered?"

"Not if he was a trader, or someone I only worked with over the phone."

Jenna looked suspicious. "Okay. So you think you might have known him. And your theory is?"

Seth wondered if he should put the crazy idea into words. "Well, I was thinking that maybe he knows that you and I..." Pausing, Seth wondered what term aptly described his and Jenna's relationship.

"Used to date?" she supplied.

Seeing as they were having a baby, "date" didn't quite seem to cover their interaction, but Seth nodded and continued, "Don't get too upset, but I wondered if the guy was trying to kidnap you to hold you for ransom."

Her jaw slackened, then she laughed abruptly. "It's not exactly like I'm an heiress, Seth." With wry humor meant to keep the demons of her own past away, she added, "and it's not as if Ralph and Nancy Robinson would fork over their life savings if I was in trouble."

Ralph and Nancy. Seth was always struck by how Jenna referred to her parents by their first names, as if to distance herself from them. "They probably would," Seth countered softly.

Jenna rolled her eyes. "Right."

"They might not have loved you enough—" As he said the words, he realized it was the first time he'd used the word love in a conversation with Jenna. "But they weren't without feelings for you."

She shrugged, masking the hurt. "Well, I doubt some guy you worked with in New York would nab me, hoping to get money out of my folks in Bear Creek, North Carolina."

Glancing from the windshield, Seth surveyed her a long moment. "I figured they'd call me."

She lifted a horrified hand to cover her mouth. "You?"

"There's a lot of money in the Tyler S&L."

Now she looked genuinely concerned. "That's what you were afraid of?"

He nodded.

Looking oddly touched, she swallowed hard. "And you'd get me out of trouble?"

He started to say he'd call Dom, since Dom was her fiancé. Or that she could hock her own diamond engagement ring for the ransom. But then he looked into her glittering green eyes and saw how they'd softened, turning as liquidly warm as the sea at night, and he could only say what he really felt. "Yes. For you, I'd give a kidnapper every last dollar in Tyler."

"YOU'D REALLY pay my ransom?" Jenna asked hours later, glancing around the master bedroom as she and Seth jointly shook out a baby blanket and placed it gently over Gretchen, who was lying on a makeshift bed of cushions on the floor.

Softly chuckling, Seth glanced up, and the way his appreciative eyes took in Jenna's one-piece green crushed-velvet lounging suit made her glad she'd changed clothes. He said, "Would I really pay your ransom? Hmm. On second thought, it would depend on the amount."

Playfully swatting his arm, she offered a quick, flirtatious smirk, masking how much his earlier words had touched her. "That's not what you said in the car."

''No. I said I'd give your kidnapper every dollar in Tyler, didn't I?''

She smiled. ''Yeah.'' When his gaze meshed with hers, the concern and veiled need she saw there sent a jolt of awareness through her. Her voice softening, she added, ''Are you less worried now that you talked to Coop?''

Seth shrugged. ''Some. He said he'd be on the lookout for a white car.''

Inadvertently, her hand moved downward, and she rubbed a splayed palm over her belly. She'd called Dom, too, and he and Sue seemed surprisingly content to have her stay in Tyler indefinitely, to talk to Seth about the baby. She sighed. ''I hate to think that someone really might be following me.''

''If so, we'll catch him. There aren't many strangers in Tyler, so he should be easy to find.'' Seth's glance warmed, softening as he stared down at Gretchen again. Clad in a yellow sleeper with her small fist tightly curled around an edge of the blanket, she was sucking sleepily on her thumb. ''She's cute, huh?'' Seth murmured.

Jenna's insides fluttered as if a hundred butterflies had just taken flight, and she sucked in a deep breath. How could she have underestimated this man? He was going to turn out to be such a good father. All night, just as in New York, he'd doted on Gretchen, teasing her, and she'd broken out in giggles as he fed her.

Seth looked luscious, too. After dinner, he'd changed into worn jeans and a soft white sweater, and now in the dim light of the bedroom, his narrowly slanted eyes looked as darkly soft as the night sky beyond the window. Just by the way he was watching Gretchen, Jenna could tell he was thinking about their baby. For hours, during dinner, they'd talked about the pregnancy—never even discussing arrangements for custody, which was what she'd expected, but only sharing their joint excitement. Jenna fought it, but a husky edge crept into her voice. "Things are going to be so great. Our baby will be…" She tried but couldn't think of a word to encompass her powerful feelings.

Seth half turned toward her, his voice lowering, becoming almost hoarse. "Do you mind?"

She frowned. "Mind?"

He shrugged. "Oh, never mind. I was just going to ask…" His voice trailed off. Obviously unwilling to pursue the conversation he'd initiated, he glanced away. Jenna did the same, her gaze inadvertently sweeping the bed, the sudden burning desire to share it with him tonight claiming her. "The furniture's the same as in New York," she murmured.

He glanced around. "Strange to see it somewhere else, huh?"

She nodded. "The house is so much bigger than your apartment that you're going to have to buy some new things."

"I figured I'd paint first."

She tried not to think of how fun it would be to decorate the place with him. "Any colors in mind?"

His gaze had settled unmistakably on her mouth,

and now he glanced up, his expression almost quizzical, as if he'd been a thousand miles away, or as if she'd suddenly spoken in a foreign language. "Uh, no. I figured white would do just fine."

She grimaced. "Boring. At least paint the molding in other colors."

He shrugged. "I thought I'd strip it and refinish the wood. Anyway, Jenna—" He thrust his hands deep into the pockets of his jeans. "I really want to take you over to my dad's tomorrow for Sunday dinner. You've already met him and my brothers, but…"

Her eyes narrowing, she surveyed him, trying not to show her surprise. "You want me to spend the day with your family?"

"Not all day," he assured. "Just a few hours."

When her heart missed a beat, she knew she'd stay weeks, even a lifetime, if Seth asked. "Sure, why not?" she managed, though she knew there were a thousand reasons why she shouldn't get drawn into Seth's world. Dom, for instance.

Only when their eyes met again did she realize she'd glanced toward the bed. He said, "Will you be all right up here?"

Her voice was droll. "All alone, you mean?"

He stared calmly at her as if to assure her that any invitation she offered, no matter how mildly flirtatious, might be taken as sincere. Aware that her rapid pulse beat was probably visible in her throat, she felt something akin to despair wash over her. Why did the simple meat-and-potatoes dinner they'd shared have to be so perfect? Why did he have to look so content as he stared down at Gretchen, his eyes so full of paternal possession? And why did he want her to spend time with his family?

For hours, she and Seth had shared their excitement about the baby, mulling over whether it would be a boy or a girl and discussing names. It had been far too easy to enter into the fantasy that Seth wasn't just excited about the baby, but about further building a relationship with her. "I'll definitely be comfortable up here." She forced a smile. "Your bed's the best." She'd been thinking about the firmness of the king-size mattress, and now color flooded her cheeks. Quickly she added, "Sure you don't mind sleeping on the couch downstairs?"

Seth shook his head. "I'm a little too tall and my feet hang over, but I'll live."

His glance was guarded, his dark eyes as expressionless as they were penetrating; his casual stance belied any emotion, but she could tell he wanted her. Both of them were silently, painfully aware that they'd never spent the night together without making love. "Well…" Jenna finally offered awkwardly, then glanced again at Gretchen.

Seth's barely audible voice seemed to drip seduction. "Cute as hell, isn't she?"

"You said that before." Her lips tilted upward. "But did you mean me or Gretchen?"

A slight bemused smile curled his lips. "Definitely Gretchen."

Jenna pouted, but the smile twitching at her lips broke through. For a second, as their eyes locked, everything seemed exactly as it used to be between them. She tried to glance toward the window, to break the connection before the recollections of their old relationship broke her heart, and yet she simply couldn't tear her eyes from his. The dim room, lit only by a standing lamp, seemed overly warm, and yet Jenna knew the heat came from inside her, or maybe from Seth's body, which wasn't a foot away. ''Well,'' she managed, ''I guess I'd better head to bed.''

He nodded. ''Sure.'' Even though he took the cue and strode abruptly toward the door, the slow burn of his parting gaze lanced into her, weakening her knees. Her lips parted, and she almost called him back to her.

As if reading her mind, he turned, pausing at the door and leaning lazily in the frame. Even though she knew she shouldn't, she was drawn to him, pulled like a moth to flame. Suddenly, she felt like an age-old gothic virgin ceaselessly melting into a dark, devastating villain's arms, mesmerized by his gaze. But Seth Spencer was no villain. Judging by his self-contained fury at the police station, he'd welcome any opportunity to protect her.

Her eyes drifted from where his white sweater pulled across broad shoulders, then down to where worn denim lovingly cupped his maleness. She offered a smile. ''I hardly ever see you in jeans. Always suits.''

He shrugged. ''We used to go out right after I got off from work.''

''When we went out.''

Male awareness sparked in Seth's eyes at her recognition of what they'd once had. Immediately the light seemed dimmer, the room smaller, his eyes drowsier. He lifted a lazy, jet eyebrow, surveying her from beneath a thick fringe of lashes. ''Thought you wanted to go to bed?''

Glancing away, she said, ''I'd better,'' even though what she really wanted was a kiss goodnight. ''Earlier,'' she began, ''when you asked me if I minded…what did you mean?''

He was watching her carefully, and the soft catch in his voice found an answering catch in her heart. ''I was going to touch you.''

Her heart was hammering. ''Touch me?''

His voice dropped a full octave, becoming silkier and more seductive than she'd ever heard it. ''I wanted to mold my hand over your belly, Jenna, to feel my baby there, growing inside you.''

She couldn't speak—words lodged in her throat—but moving on impulse, she took his hand, overturned it and pressed his palm to her belly, then she glided her own hand over the back of his. ''There,'' she whispered.

His caressing gaze dropped as his fingers carefully traced velvet, probing the softness of her belly. ''So soft,'' he murmured as she came another step closer, almost into his arms.

''I can't feel anything yet,'' she whispered, near enough now that scents of his cologne came with her breath. ''It'll be a while before the baby kicks.''

She barely heard Seth's voice. "Are you sick?"

She shook her head, touched by his sincere expression, and by how his eyes, no less than his huge broad hands, stroked the space beneath which their baby lay. "No. Not yet," she said, sharply inhaling. "Maybe I'll be lucky and I won't."

She could see how hard his throat worked when he swallowed. "Amazing," he whispered.

"Amazing?"

He nodded, his eyes now drifting up to hers. "You and I made a baby, Jen."

She'd known that, of course. But feeling Seth's breath fan so delicately against her cheek as he whispered the truth of it, truly unsettled her. All at once, it became totally, magically real. "Bet she'll have your eyes."

"Bet he'll have your nose."

A slight smile curled the mouth he'd always said was her best feature. "Your hands."

"Your mouth," he countered.

"You always did like that part of me," she returned, unable to help the huskiness that claimed the words.

His voice was even huskier. "I liked all of you, Jenna."

"Liked? As in past tense?"

"I'd like you better, if you weren't getting married."

With the father of her coming child so close, she was powerless but to follow the call of her heart. "You could always stop me."

They were dangerous words. "Would you let me?"

Yes. It was on the tip of her tongue, but she decided to wait and see what he had to say. After all, only this morning, she'd been ready to marry another man. "My lips are sealed."

"Sealed?" A slight smile quirked his mouth as he shook his head. "No," he whispered, "your lips are something else entirely."

"Such as?"

"Dangerous."

So were his. They weren't but five inches away, and as Seth tilted his head another breathless fraction, her eyes settled on the soft cleft in his strong chin. Suddenly, it and every other small detail about him did unstoppable, crazy things to her heart. His shoulders were so wide, the enticing thatch of black, tangled hair swirling near the open throat of his sweater so unspeakably soft, and the strong hand Seth had splayed on her rib cage was now flexing, as if registering how fast her heart was hammering. He leaned forward. Just as she registered the brush of soft denim against her thighs, she inhaled and his strong male scent slid into her head, making her giddy, and then she was in his arms.

"Those lips," he murmured, licking his own and leaning so they almost touched hers as his eyes strayed hungrily down, settling on the target.

"Dangerous, you said?" she murmured.

"Lethal," he assured just as his mouth settled, his top lip nestling between hers, his bottom curling petulantly in a slow, hot kiss he'd obviously wanted all night, one that built in seconds to more sumptuous heat than either of them had bargained for. Not that they stopped. Her hands had a life of their own, gliding upward on his sweater, its very softness attesting to its being of cashmere, the very hardness beneath attesting to the fact that Seth Spencer wanted her badly. He was hard elsewhere, too, straining his jeans, his erection pressing the belly that held their child.

Breathlessly she sighed as his tongue plunged, then swirled inside her mouth, making her heart ache and the tips of her breasts almost hurt with the need for his intimate caress. Heat burst inside her, then spread, coating the surface of her skin. ''What are we doing, Seth?'' she murmured against his mouth.

His voice was a deep growl. ''Kissing.''

There was no denying that. It was deep and hard and wet. ''You know what I mean.''

He leaned back a fraction, not so far that she couldn't still feel his breath, then his eyes slowly caressed her face, lingering on her swollen, kiss-slackened mouth. ''We're going to sleep,'' he whispered, touching his lips to hers once more. ''And tomorrow, we're going to my father's. And then...''

She raised her eyes, searching his. ''And then?''

''We'll see,'' he said.

With that, he brushed a thumb lightly over the lips he'd so lovingly kissed, and then he was gone.

Chapter Nine

"Jenna's really something, Seth," Elias Spencer said the next day, clapping his son on the shoulder. "Pretty as a picture and sharp as a tack." Softly chuckling, Elias hiked a pant leg, wedged a foot against a porch step, then stared into the backyard. "And she's pregnant. I swear, I never thought I'd see a grandchild around here."

"Came as a surprise to me, too," Seth admitted, his heart pulling.

"Everybody in church was doting on little Gretchen."

Seth nodded. "I was afraid she'd cry, but she snoozed instead."

Elias laughed. "And the roof didn't cave in when you walked inside. Who'd you bribe? Saint Peter?"

Seth grinned as he thrust his hands deep into the trouser pockets of a steel-gray suit he'd worn to the service. "It's definitely been awhile since I saw the inside of a church."

"Hmm. It didn't cave in on Jenna, either."

Another throaty laugh carried on a gust of autumn

breeze as Seth thought about Jenna's grand entrance into the Tyler Fellowship Sanctuary, wearing a zebra-print dress and combat boots. "It might not have caved in, but I thought some members of the Baron and Trask families might faint when they saw her."

Elias grinned. "Tyler's best families have undoubtedly seen more scandalous things than Jenna."

"Best families usually have." As he said the words, Seth's heart unexpectedly squeezed. His father's presence, the sharp autumn air and the scent of Sunday turkey wafting through the open door reminded him of the day his mother left.

Oblivious of his thoughts, Elias said, "I sure had to fan myself with the hymnal when Jenna waltzed in."

Seth's smile returned. "Everybody got a kick out of her."

"Well, things sure do change," sighed the older man, his eyes suddenly seeming far away. "After all these years, I still can't believe we've got a lady preacher."

"Chauvinist."

Elias shrugged. "Maybe, but Reverend Sarah writes a good sermon, doesn't she? I don't know about you, but it made me feel all warm and fuzzy."

Seth laughed. "She was trying to make you feel repentant, not warm and fuzzy, Dad."

Elias chuckled. "Repentant? Not me," he assured. "Not while there's so much sin in the world to enjoy."

Seth smiled, somehow doubting that Reverend

Sarah's message about loving your brother could do much to quell the rampant gossip around town. He still wasn't sure if Caroline Benning had called him about Jenna's pregnancy, but the news had apparently leaked and spread. This morning Tyler's quilting circle had claimed a full pew, and Tillie Phelps, Martha Bauer and Kaitlin Rodier had spent the service whispering behind their hankies while staring at Seth and Jenna.

Now Seth glanced toward the kitchen window, through which he could see Jenna helping Eva, Elias's housekeeper, do the dishes. The domestic vision did strange things to Seth's insides, as did having Sunday dinner at the big Victorian home on Maple Street where he'd grown up. Reaching into the breast pocket of his suit, he pulled out two cigars, tilting one in his father's direction.

Elias shook his head. "I'll pass. Let my dinner settle."

"It was a good meal," Seth agreed, exchanging a quick, satisfied glance with his father.

Striking a match, Seth lit the tip of an imported cigar, drawing on pungent smoke that warmed his mouth as surely as Jenna's kiss last night, then he stared from the porch into the backyard, where Quinn and Brady were hunkered down on their hands and knees, growling playfully like dogs and chasing Gretchen, who was crawling through the grass.

Elias frowned. "Hate to see them scaring that little one."

Seth merely chuckled, staring past his brothers to

the lush farmlands beyond the yard. "Gretchen loves it. Besides, it's warmed up a little today. Living in New York, she doesn't get much of a chance to play outside. There's a play area on the fenced-in roof of their apartment building, so she plays there, but Sue doesn't take her to the public parks. She's too afraid she'll get snatched."

"A shame," said Elias. "Kids should have a yard. Trees."

Seth tried to ignore the sense of dread stealing over him. "New York's got a lot to offer a kid," he forced himself to say, thinking of Jenna's return home. "There's the Central Park Zoo, the Botanical Gardens in the Bronx…" His voice trailed off.

"Heard she's going back," Elias offered.

Realizing his eyes had fixed on the horizon, Seth refocused them. "Huh?"

Elias blew out an angry sigh, then he suddenly leaned, resting an elbow against the porch rail. "You know exactly what I'm talking about Seth. Everybody in Tyler knows about her comings and goings."

Seth was at a loss. "Whose?"

"Jenna's!" Elias exploded. "The quilting circle at Worthington House are all saying she's marrying some man from New York. Do you mind telling me what's going on?"

Raising an eyebrow, Seth took the cigar from between his lips and tipped the ash into the yard, feeling vaguely awkward since he and Elias rarely talked about women. "Well, like everyone around town says, she's getting married."

"And not to you."

Seth shook his head.

Elias sucked angrily on his inner cheek. "I wasn't going to say anything today, but all during dinner, I could see the way you were looking at her. Every time she needed more water, you were filling her glass, or ladling more food onto her plate, or helping her feed Gretchen. You love that woman, don't you?"

Seth merely eyed his father.

"Are you really going to let her leave this town?" Elias continued. "And while she's carrying your child? What the hell are you thinking, son?"

Seth's throat tightened. He didn't like discussing his personal business with anyone, least of all his father. Sighing, he took a drag from the cigar, then exhaled a long steady stream of smoke, wondering how much to say, since Elias forbade discussions about Seth's mother. "I don't know, Dad," he finally began. "Jenna's a city woman, you know."

"City people settle here all the time," argued Elias. "I moved us all here from New York, and now you, Quinn and Brady have all come back to Tyler." When Seth said nothing, Elias blew out another frustrated sigh. "I know we never talk about your mother around here," he said, "And I know you're thinking about how she couldn't adapt to small town life…" Elias let his voice trail off and shook his head.

It was a more heartfelt speech than Seth had ever heard his father deliver, so he said what had long been on his mind. "I don't know how you feel about this, Dad, but I'd like to look for her. I want to know why she left Tyler the way she did, never even calling us.'' Seth raised a staying hand, not wanting to be interrupted. ''Over the years, I've thought of every conceivable reason she didn't stay in touch, but I'd like to hear the truth from her. Sometimes, I've thought that if that was resolved, I could start a future with Jenna.''

Elias nodded and, without asking, slipped a hand inside his son's breast pocket, taking the cigar that had been previously offered. ''Mind?''

Seth shook his head. ''I offered it, didn't I?''

Lighting the cigar, Elias nodded, exhaling the thick, aromatic smoke on a sigh. ''Ah,'' he said with satisfaction, ''this one came from Havana.'' Pausing, he glanced around the yard, then continued. ''If you're asking for my approval, you got it.'' He took a deep, thoughtful breath. ''Anyway, finding Violet might help you feel ready to start your future, but you seem to be forgetting that Jenna's already planning hers. Not to mention the future of your coming child. Everybody's talking about that wedding gown she brought to town with her. Another man loves her, wants to marry her, and wants to raise your baby.'' Elias toed the porch a moment. ''Hell,'' he finally muttered. ''You know I don't usually have this kind of father-knows-best conversation. You boys have always been free to live your lives as you see fit, but it seems to me, that with regard to Jenna, you're running out of time.''

HIS FATHER WAS right, Seth thought hours later as he and Jenna cruised through Tyler in his Blazer. After

Sunday supper they'd walked back from his father's house, watched some television, then decided to take Gretchen for a drive.

"Dinner with your family was fun," Jenna was saying, rifling a hand through her hair and pushing it off her forehead as she drew her feet beneath her in the seat.

She'd laughed and joked with Quinn and Brady as if she'd known them for years, and now Seth felt more tangled emotion than he should have. Somehow, Jenna seemed so right for Tyler; she might not know it, but she fit here like a hand in a tight glove. The evening drive through Tyler had been her idea, and now Seth's desire for her mixed with anticipation, hope and worry. "I thought you hated small towns."

Jenna laughed. "It was dinner I said I liked, not Tyler."

Seth fought disappointment, staring through the windshield. Tyler was a far cry from New York, but as they drove beneath a canopy of trees, he thought it looked glorious. Why couldn't she admire it? Red evening sunlight burst through golden leaves and, with the window down, he could hear a rippling, rustling breeze. "So, you don't like Tyler, then?"

Her bubbling laughter had tempered to a soft chuckle. "I didn't say that, either, Seth."

Now she was just teasing him. "Well, what do you think of it?" When he glanced over at her, the whole world seemed to stop. It was as if someone had taken a snapshot. For a second the moment was frozen, stopped in time. The next thing Seth knew, he was driving on automatic pilot, his eyes having left the windshield to fix on where the sun hit her hair, turning it the same red-brown as the leaves. Her smile was wide, genuine, her gorgeous green eyes lively, dancing slits. The cavalier red scarf draping her zebra-print dress gave her an exotic flair that he knew would always pull him like a magnet. She said, "You want to know what I think of Tyler, Wisconsin, huh?"

He turned his attention to the road, got his bearings, then looked at her again. This time their eyes locked, the energy between them so strong that it stole his breath. She damn well knew what he was really asking. Was she changing her mind? Did she think she could stay in a town such as this? Would she give up Dom? "Yeah," he murmured, his voice growing husky. "What do you think of Tyler?"

The emotion in her eyes deepened, softening them. "I love it, Seth. It…looks like a good place to raise a family." And then, suddenly laughing, she added, "You're looking at me as if you're starstruck. As much as I love that kind of male attention, you'd better watch the road."

He shifted his eyes back to the windshield, feeling as if she'd fastened wide bands around his torso and was now squeezing his chest. *She likes Tyler.* She liked his family, too, and she was looking forward to the baby. His heart missing a beat, he remembered how it had felt to curl his hand over her belly last night. Amazing, he'd thought. Only inches away, a child that would belong to them had begun to grow.

No matter what happened, Seth was tied to Jenna for a lifetime. There would be graduations and a confirmation. He'd be in and out of New York to visit their child. He glanced toward her, but when he saw her expression, the smile tracing his lips vanished. "What's wrong?"

"Slow down," she offered in such an urgent whisper that whatever she was warning him about could have been in the car with them.

His eyes scanned the windshield, but he saw no danger. He'd expected to see the man in the white car. "What's wrong, Jen?" he repeated.

"Just slow down."

Taking his foot off the gas pedal, Seth swerved toward the curb. The houses were modest and well-maintained, with wide porches and freshly mowed lawns. Plump, lit-up Halloween jack-o'-lanterns flickered in some of the windows, and two nearby lampposts were tied with black-and-orange bows.

Jenna scooted closer in the seat and pointed through the windshield. "Look," she said. "It's Stew Cary."

"That must be his house." He was coming down the porch steps with a football tucked under his arm. Seth loosed a soft wolf's whistle, letting the Blazer idle beneath the blowing, hanging fronds of a willow tree as he threw the car into park and reached for his seat belt. "And that's the guy who's following you. I can't believe it. The two are about to play catch."

Jenna's hand curled over his arm. "Don't get out."

Seth frowned. "Why not? Are you crazy? We've been looking for this guy for two days."

"But he's staying with Stew."

"He's supposed to be one of the good guys," Seth muttered. "A cop. No wonder he was hellbent on not taking our statement. Obviously, he's protecting this friend of his. But why was he following you?"

"I don't know, but let's go back to your place and call Cooper Night Hawk again. Stew's working for him. Maybe we've got this all wrong. I think it's better to let Cooper approach Stew."

No doubt she thought so because she was registering the powerfully dark emotion in Seth's eyes. Seth sighed. "I hate leaving now that we found him."

She shrugged. "There's nothing to be gained by approaching him ourselves. He'll just deny he was following me. And Stew will offer some excuse for not identifying a man in a white car with a red handlebar mustache as his friend."

Seth's jaw was tight, and now his cheek quivered. "You think Cooper will get more information?"

Jenna's hand relaxed over his arm. "I'm sure of it, Seth."

He watched through the windshield. As Stew ran a few paces backward in the yard, tossing the football to the redhead, Seth forced himself to put the Blazer's gear back into drive. Jenna was right. It went totally against Seth's grain, but a showdown in Stew Carey's yard wouldn't accomplish anything. Besides, just as before, Seth didn't particularly want to risk a fight while Jenna and Gretchen were in the car. He hesitated another moment. It seemed crazy to leave this guy here, after he'd already been chased through the town square and from the airport. Still, he looked as if he might be at Stew Cary's for a while. And knowing Jenna, if Seth wound up in a fight, she'd leap out and try to defend him. "Okay," he finally agreed. "We'll do it your way and call Coop."

Chapter Ten

"I can't believe Gretchen and I are still here," Jenna whispered an hour later as she finished arranging her dresses in the master bedroom's spacious walk-in closet. But why was she making herself so comfortable in Tyler? Why had she told Sue that she and Seth had a few more things to hash out about the coming baby and that she could only return to New York after that?

"Because Seth and I really aren't through talking," Jenna whispered on a sigh. It *did* look as if she were moving into Seth's closet—and house—for good, though. She'd overpacked, as always, and now she'd lined the myriad suitcases in a corner, so the bedroom wouldn't look quite so cluttered. Unlike her, Seth was always as neat as a pin. Wistfully tracing a hand over the white fabric of the wedding dress she'd brought to town, she thought about Seth's grim expression as he'd carried it inside. A smile drifted across her lips as she recalled how he'd held the dress—out from his body with a finger hooked around the hanger as if the whole mess were something he'd prefer to deposit in the trash, not his closet.

Now her heart fluttered. She had no idea what was going through his mind right now, but Seth definitely didn't want her leaving town, or to see her walking down the aisle wearing this gorgeous dress for Dom. "But I'm going to," she firmly told herself. She wasn't merely hanging around Tyler waiting for a proposal from Seth Spencer. "Hell, no," she suddenly vowed with a soft curse. "That's not what I'm doing here." Jenna Robinson was definitely made of tougher stuff.

Just as she'd informed Sue, she simply had no choice but to stay here. She'd take things on a day-by-day basis and when Sue got antsy about seeing Gretchen, she'd head back to New York. She couldn't leave while she and Seth still had so many things to discuss about the baby, could she? On a rush of pique, she further reminded herself that she'd sworn she'd leave Tyler with her dignity intact. Sure, she'd stayed here—even been motivated to come here, if she were honest—in order to give Seth a chance to revive their relationship, but mild flirtation, two shared kisses, or a talk about his abandonment issues with his mother hardly marked the road to marriage, any more than did having Sunday dinner with his family or wild sex on a desktop. No, Dom's insistence she visit Tyler wasn't really her only reason for doing so, as she'd previously convinced herself, but now she was hard-pressed to see what she'd accomplished, except for telling Seth he was going to be a daddy.

Jenna's shoulder lifted in an involuntary shrug as sadness twisted inside her. She and Seth had always shared unspeakable passion, but now she needed commitment. She was touched by Seth's response to the pregnancy, glad he wanted to be a part of their baby's life, but hadn't he understood a full-time father was needed?

She sighed, her parents drifting through her mind once more. This time around, Jenna really was through with begging for love, and Seth had had ample opportunity—both in New York and in Tyler—to ask her to share his life. She'd been over the issues with herself a thousand times, hadn't she? Why couldn't she let go and accept that it didn't matter how much she liked Tyler, any more than how delightful she found Seth's father and brothers, or the fact that the baby growing inside her belonged to Seth.

"And Dom," she murmured, her eyebrows knitting. This evening Jenna had called him and was surprised when Sue had answered. Dom hadn't even bothered to come to the phone. He'd been too busy, making tandoori chicken, which was his specialty, and Sue hadn't seemed to mind in the least that Gretchen would be gone another day or two. As relieved as Jenna felt, it seemed odd for Sue to take this continued separation from her daughter so lightly. Jenna expected her to be upset by now. It was almost as if Sue and Dom were enjoying having this time to themselves. Uneasily, Jenna wondered if Dom really missed her.

"Oh, please," she muttered. "Why shouldn't he

spend time with Sue? We've all been friends for
years. Besides, I'm here with Seth. Talk about the pot
calling the kettle black.''

Her throat tightened and, unbidden, the image of
the Tyler Fellowship Sanctuary came into her mind.
There she was: wearing the wedding dress she'd
brought, lifting her satin-clad feet and taking small
steps down a long white runner toward the altar, her
fingers curled around a bouquet of white and pink
roses, and her eyes on Seth who was waiting for her
in his tux.

Should she go downstairs? she wondered, glancing
toward the door. Maybe pretend she was craving a
midnight snack from the kitchen? Or that she wanted
to check on Gretchen, who'd looked so comfortable
asleep in an armchair that Jenna and Seth had agreed
to leave her there? Sighing, unable to decide, Jenna
lifted the hem of her zebra-print dress, pulled it over
her shoulders and hung it up, then slipped off her bra.
Opening a suitcase, she rustled through it for a
nightie. ''The blue one?'' she murmured. She lifted a
low-cut shortie gown, surveyed it, then discarded it
in favor of a new confection made of emerald-green
silk with rhinestone-studded spaghetti straps.

She was still busy tugging it down when she
stepped from the closet into the darkened room and
headed for the bed. The low, barely audible husky
voice sounding near her ear startled her. ''Nice,'' he
said. ''Very nice.''

''Seth?'' Her heart hammered with surprise, and
her bare feet stilled on the thick carpet. Squinting into

the darkness, she was barely able to make out his features in the light shining in from the hallway.

"None other."

He seemed unusually still, standing scarcely a foot from the bed and not moving a muscle. Although he was still in the trousers he'd worn to church, he'd removed his shirt, and in the dim light, his broad shadowy shoulders and muscular bare chest made him look so powerful that she found herself shuddering.

"Cold?" he purred.

He knew very well she wasn't. Dammit, she thought, her legs turning rubbery, would she ever get over wanting him? She felt like she was standing on two overcooked noodles. Trying her best not to look affected, she came within a foot of him before she realized her hand was still pressed over her heart. Beneath her fingertips, it felt like a beat played by a wild, primitive drummer, loudly thudding out of control. Unable to help herself, she shot him a Cheshire cat's smile, then lifted a long slender finger and ran a nail between his pectorals, eliciting the same shudder from him which she'd just experienced. "My," she murmured, chuckling softly. "I guess you're cold, too." That would serve him right.

He merely shrugged, a slight, flirtatious smile lifting his lips. "Either that, or I'm all hot and bothered."

"Cold, I'm sure," she countered.

"You're probably right," he returned mildly. "It's the Wisconsin weather, no doubt."

"Must be. Tyler *is* a racy town."

Seth nodded. "Nothing like the nightlife."

Everything in his eyes said *she* was the nightlife. Although she tried to modulate her tone, her raw anticipation was unmistakable even when she switched the subject. "What are you doing up here, anyway?" she managed. "Did you get a call from Cooper?"

Seth's lower lip curled in obvious disappointment at the change in topic, and he didn't bother to hide the fact that his eyes had drifted slowly to the low scooping neckline of her nightie, settling where her breasts were nearly exposed. He shook his head. "Nope. Coop still hasn't called back. I don't understand it. So far, all I've gotten is his machine."

"Well, you promised me you wouldn't go back over to Stew Cary's tonight. You won't, will you?"

Seth looked none too happy. "The guy's probably not even there anymore."

"Even if he was, you know he wouldn't tell you the truth about whether or not he was following me, and you said Cooper Night Hawk's a great cop, so I'm sure he'll get to the bottom of this. If Stew Cary was protecting the guy for some reason, Cooper will figure out why, too. Meantime…" Her breath caught.

Seth arched an eyebrow. "Do you have something in mind?"

Many things. Seth was close enough that she could smell his skin, and the deep breath she intentionally inhaled did exactly what she intended it to do— brought a scent so male, tangy and arousing that her toes curled into the carpet. As she glanced over his naked hairy chest, everything she'd been thinking earlier flew from her mind. She no longer felt as if she was a thousand miles from home, or as if she was headed back to work at the gallery in a few days. Dom ceased to exist. So did her responsibility to get Gretchen back to Sue. Before she thought it through, her voice dropped again, becoming a faint rasp. "Meantime…" The word echoed in her mind. Looking into his eyes, she'd completely forgotten what she intended to say. She was suddenly aware that only a scant piece of silk covered her. Lamely, she finished. "I'm sure we'll talk to him soon."

Eyeing her with obvious interest, Seth said, "I guess. *If* we answer the phone."

Clearly, he wanted to take it off the hook. Jenna's voice sounded shaky to her own ears. "Is Gretchen okay?"

"Sleeping like a baby. No pun intended."

Jenna swallowed hard. "Look, Seth, I don't think we should—"

The next thing she knew he'd closed the distance between them. His thigh brushed hers, the coarse fabric of his dress slacks roughening her bare skin. Leaning and twining their fingers, he brought her hand to his chest, making her heart miss beats as wildly tangled chest hairs glided against her skin. Seth's voice lowered to a rumble that stirred her blood. "I'm tired of hearing what I should and shouldn't do, Jenna."

She sucked in a quavering breath. There was no use defending against him. Already, molten heat had curled through her limbs, gathering in a searingly tight knot at the core of her. Her lips parted in unspoken protest, as if against the sheer force of what she felt, and she felt the lulling, insistent warmth inside her spread ever so slowly to her cheeks…then to her neck…then to her breasts. His eyes had dropped again, the gaze as hungry, penetrating and effective as a touch to her naked skin. When her nipples puckered in response, he whispered, ''You've got the power, Jen. But why deny us both tonight?''

A shiver zipped down her spine just as unmet need and something akin to panic turned her insides jumpy. Instinctively, she tried to step back, away from him. ''You know it's not that easy, Seth,'' she managed when he didn't let go of her hand, but only held it immobile against the wall of his chest, tightening the fingers he'd twined through hers. ''When we're done talking about how we're going to handle things in the future with the baby, you know I'm going back to New York.''

His eyes were flitting between her mouth and the bare skin of her shoulders and, ignoring her words, he hooked a finger beneath a strap of her gown, easing it downward, nearly baring a nipple. ''The future?'' he murmured. ''Right now it's the present that seems important.''

Her breath felt cut off, completely short-circuited. ''Please…we need to talk about how we're going to handle the baby…''

Seth edged the strap down another fraction. ''Maybe, but some of the best conversations are silent.''

No breath was left in her body now. Her heart was

pounding so hard against her rib cage that she could hear the beat hammering in her ears. Whatever thoughts were in her mind seemed like mere nonsensical fragments. Seth had done nothing more than touch her bare skin, but she was throbbing, aching between her legs for what she knew only he could offer. It didn't seem fair. Why couldn't she love Dom—or at least fight Seth? "Please," she said, the words coming out in a whisper, sounding broken. "What do you want from me, Seth?"

"Want?"

"Yes, want." He knew what she meant. She'd committed to Dom and yet Seth was claiming her body in a way he knew she could never deny. It wasn't fair to any of them. She was a good person. She wanted to treat Dom right. And yet, right now nothing—and no one—existed for her except Seth Spencer.

In the dark room, his darker eyes had turned to narrowed slits of need the color of midnight, and his voice, in the silence, was rough with seduction as he lowered the strap of her gown once more, this time far enough that the beaded, wanting tip of another breast was exposed. "Rosy," he murmured.

"Seth," she warned.

"You know what I want." His tone deepened. "And, Jenna," he added, his gaze lingering on her taut nipple, "by the looks of it, I'd say you want it, too."

Why couldn't she simply move away from him?

she wondered, fighting to keep her knees from buckling. "I'm marrying Dom," she protested.

Seth's words came like a snake through tall grass, soft and dangerous. "Like hell you are."

Her voice was strangled, hopeful. "I'm not?"

Seth didn't bother to answer, but simply lowered his mouth, locking it over the tight hard bud he'd exposed, eliciting a sharp, involuntary cry from her. Her mind spun. It burst apart, then cracked into slivers as heady need for him shot through her, followed by dangerous, uncontrollable emotion that simply crashed headlong into her bloodstream. Dropping back her head, she was powerless but to offer total surrender. Just as her knees gave out, Seth's strong arm wrapped around her back supporting her. Staring blindly at the ceiling, she gasped, allowing his warm silken tongue to plunge her into ecstasy.

HER TASTE REMINDED Seth of winter spices such as cinnamon and nutmeg, and as he palmed both breasts, swirling his tongue in wet circles around a straining nipple, he leaned into Jenna, pressing both his hard thighs to hers. Wedging a raised knee between her long bare legs, he felt them part for him and released a throaty groan.

"Ah," he whispered. That was Jenna. Always opening for him with the ease of water. If she'd been thinking about Dom earlier tonight, her current expression of sweet surrender said she'd forgotten him now. With each touch and kiss, Seth silently vowed to make her forget Dom forever, to use this chance to remind her of what they'd always shared.

"Baby…sweetheart…Jenna," he pattered huskily, his erection flexing as swift need coursed through him. With raw desire flooding into his extremities, he masterfully turned her in his arms, the feel of the long delicate curve of her back doing outrageous things to his heartbeat. His throat closed with emotion. She was so tall. So slender. So gorgeous. And right now, regardless of whom she claimed she was about to marry, she was his. She was the mother of his coming child. The woman he was about to take.

He walked her the scant remaining foot to the bed until her knees hit the back of the mattress, then he simply sprawled with her, arms and legs tangling. His eyes, heavy-lidded and glazed with lust, fixed hungrily on hers as he thrust a hand deeply into her hair, his groin pulling once more as the silky strands teased the spaces between his fingers. In the darkness, her glittering eyes were the same deep emerald green as the quilted duvet and the nightie she wore.

Reaching downward, he drummed his fingertips at the hem, tracing circles on her thigh, then he flattened his palm, pushing the gown upward, gliding it over the full round curve of her hip to the sweet dip of her waist, the silk feeling cool, his thumb hot as it brushed her unclothed skin. Pausing, he shifted his hand, splaying it, widening his fingers over her still-flat belly as he brought his lips to the curve of her ear, whispering, "We're having a baby, Jen. Can you believe it?"

The soft catch of her voice was nearly lost to the shadowy darkness. "Not really. No. No, I don't feel like I'll really believe this until he or she is in my arms."

"My arms, too."

"Yes," she whispered dreamily. "Your arms."

His eyes had settled on the long slender column of her exposed throat where the pulse beat was moving rapidly back and forth, like a strobe. "Stay with me, Jen."

He barely heard her response. "The baby needs a father."

"I'm the father."

Before she could respond, need crowded Seth's senses again, overtaking them, leaving him powerless but to bring his mouth crushing down on hers in a swooping, devouring, hard deep kiss that had her shifting her weight as if she were fighting not to writhe against him. But writhe she would. He'd make sure of that. Gasping, he continued pushing the sexy nightie upward, whispering, "This looks good on you, but I'd rather see it off."

"I'm getting that impression."

If his heart hadn't been pounding so hard, he would have smiled. But he couldn't, not when he pushed yet another inch of silk northward, now gliding over her full breasts. His eyes intense and passionate, he looked his fill, his searing gaze lingering on each distended dusky bud, then suddenly he lowered himself, his whole body aching for her as he kissed each one, flicking the tip of his tongue here then there, feeling the turgid peaks further knot in his mouth, bursting with the taste of pure pleasure. Deeper, more silkily, he drew her between his lips, nibbling until she was twining both hands in his hair.

He loved feeling her nails swirling against his scalp, and the soft brush of her lips in his hair, and how she whispered strangled, nonsensical incantations into the strands. Her legs further parted, allowing him access, and as he finished drawing the gown over her head and tossing it to the floor, he angled himself closer.

"I know I've said it before," he began hoarsely, the aroused part of him settling with nothing between them now but his trousers and some red next-to-nothing thong panties that she wore for the same reason she wore all her exotic clothes—to drive him wild.

"Said what?"

Lifting a finger, he brushed a strand of hair from her temple. "That every last inch of you seems calculated to drive me to distraction," he murmured, his eyes enjoying the play of light on her shoulders as a warm rosy flush spread over her exposed, lust-warmed skin.

"You're not so bad yourself."

"Jenna." His voice suddenly seemed to come from outside himself, wrenched from him on a surge of emotion. "Jenna," he said again, this time growling her name, his ravenous gaze heading southward, moving like a brushfire, searing down her body and not stopping until he'd leaned away to view the small patch of red silk panty curving her mound. His heart stuttering, he brushed a hand over the soft fabric, feeling the tangled curls before molding a palm over an equally silken buttock. A fast shudder rippling down his back, he reached between their bodies, grappling with his belt and zipper while she looked on, lightly licking lips that had parted in anticipation.

"Like hell you're going back to New York, Jen," he whispered right before his lips fastened to hers, locking on her mouth with a surety that said they belonged together. Plunging his tongue between her open lips, he felt another wave of undeniable need claim him as he rid himself of his slacks. She moaned as he slid next to her again, now skin to skin, heat to heat, need to need. Out of habit, he started to reach for a condom in the drawer of the bedside table, then he realized she was already pregnant.

"Dom," he suddenly found himself murmuring into her hair. "I'm going to make you forget him."

She sounded lost. "You fool," she murmured back. "I never slept with him."

Not bothering to mask his shock, Seth slid closer, his arousal resting where she most wanted him, his voice gruff with need. "Really? Is that true, Jen?"

"Do I lie?"

"No."

"He heard me talking on the phone with the doctor and he proposed…"

Everything in her voice said she wasn't in love with the man they both knew as a friend. Suddenly, what Seth had felt since her arrival in Tyler came to the fore and his voice broke. "Why'd you say yes?"

Their gazes meshed and held, and she shivered as if with renewed awareness of their naked bodies and that he was poised to enter her. "You weren't there, Seth."

"I'm here now."

A tremble of a smile curled her lips. "Me, too."

And she was, he thought. Right where she should be—warm and naked in his bed. "I want you to think about something, Jen."

Sliding her hands over his biceps, she curled them around his bare shoulders. "What?"

"Think about marrying me instead." The words seemed to leave her speechless, so he added in a raspy, seductive whisper, "Why don't you let me convince you?" And then he guided himself to her, entering her with a deliciously slow, deliberate thrust, an endlessly hot stroke that wrenched from her a high-pitched sharp cry and one solitary word: his name.

Chapter Eleven

"Jen?"

Yawning, Seth snuggled further down in bed, raising a hand to dreamily scratch his chest. After a moment, he glided it downward, found where the duvet had bunched around his knees, drew it to his waist, then slitted open his eyes a fraction, just enough to let in sunlight. Everything in the room seemed strangely still. Bursts of gold, red and orange leaves were framed in a window he'd cracked open last night and now, as he listened to their rustling and some chirping birds, he drew a lungful of fresh autumn air and decided he could live a million years and never get used to waking up in Tyler. After seven weeks without blaring taxi horns and sirens, Seth was positive he'd never get over the unsettling feeling he'd landed on another planet. *Definitely,* he thought, cracking a smile. *I feel like I've come to Tyler via Mars or Jupiter. Or maybe Venus, given the fact that Jen's beside me in bed.*

His smile broadened. Had he really asked her to

marry him? His mind replayed the words: *I want you to think about something, Jen.*

What?

Think about marrying me.

Last night she hadn't answered. Hell, Seth hadn't given her the opportunity. Every time she started to talk, he'd parted her lips with his own and kissed her until they were making love again. Afterward, they'd brought Gretchen up to bed and fallen asleep with her between them, exhausted. How could Seth have fooled himself into thinking he could live without Jenna? Was he out of his mind?

On a sigh, he realized Jenna would say yes to his proposal this morning. She wasn't in love with Dom, she hadn't even slept with him—something that relieved Seth immeasurably—and last night she'd made love to Seth with a passion that surpassed any they'd previously shared.

Yes, Jenna Robinson would accept his proposal of marriage this morning. What a way to start a day. "Hey, Jen," he whispered, still not fully opening his eyes, "are you missing the roar of the subway?"

When there was no answer, he glanced away from the early morning sunlight, realizing she was no longer in bed with him. It was only eight o'clock, and Jenna never got up this early unless she'd set an alarm. Even then, getting her to open her eyes and sip a cup of coffee could be a chore. And where was Gretchen? Seth sat upright, blinking and thrusting a hand through hair that Jenna had left unforgivably disheveled. Still smiling, he recalled how her fingers felt raking across his scalp, then his heart swelled inside his chest. Jenna was having his baby. For a while last night, they'd slept like spoons, with both his hands molding over her belly. Even better, he was sure they'd be sleeping together every night from now on. Maybe he'd fly back to New York with her, to take Gretchen home and help pack Jenna's belongings for the move to Tyler.

But where was she now?

All at once, his smile vanished and he whisked back the covers; the redheaded man in the white car flashed through his mind. For the briefest instant Seth was sure he'd been right. The man really was after Jenna. Maybe he'd kidnapped her and Gretchen and was about to call for ransom. "Calm down," he muttered to himself. Jenna was probably right. He was getting paranoid. No doubt, just as she'd tried to convince him before, seeing the redheaded man so often was merely a coincidence. Still, Seth wished Cooper Night Hawk had returned his call.

"Jenna?" he called out, fighting concern. "Jen? Where are you?"

The shower? Probably, he thought with relief, nothing more than the idea making his groin tighten. Maybe he should join her. Chocking his head and straining to hear the running water, he stared a long moment at the indentation her head had left in the pillow. Then he realized she couldn't be in the shower; she wouldn't have taken Gretchen with her unless she was giving the baby a bath.

He yelled, "Are you downstairs, Jen?"

Silence met his ears. So much for hoping she'd decided to fix him breakfast in bed. For a second, Seth had actually been entertaining the notion that Jenna was in the kitchen, stark naked except for an apron, fixing him eggs and bacon. But he knew Jenna better than that. Oh, she'd happily wear an apron over her bare buns, but even when food came tidily wrapped in take-out bags, she could barely be bothered to re-heat it. In their relationship, Seth had always been the cook.

"Jen?"

Heaving a sigh and throwing back the covers, he got up, strode toward the window and stared down at the driveway, his lips parting in astonishment. "Wait a minute," he muttered. "She took the Blazer. But where—"

The airport!

"Dammit," he cursed. Turning, he glanced quickly around the room. None of her belongings were here. Why hadn't he noticed before? "She's gone back to New York," he whispered. The knowledge washed over him like cold ice. Without questioning it, he knew it was true. He hadn't fought hard enough for Jenna's love, and she'd decided to marry Dom. Didn't that explain why she hadn't answered Seth's proposal last night?

For a second he merely stood there, stunned, then his body began doing what it always had in a crisis— moving. Grabbing his trousers, he stepped into them. He shoved a hand deep into a pocket, futilely fumbling around folded dollar bills and coins for his car keys—and was reminded once more that Jenna had taken his only vehicle.

"I should have known," he muttered, his muscles tense as he headed downstairs for his shirt and shoes. What was he supposed to do now? Should he follow her? Borrow his father's car? Or maybe Quinn or Brady's? Or should he stay put instead? Suddenly, Seth felt like the worst kind of fool for wanting to chase her. She was a grown woman. She could make her own decisions.

"She ought to do so without stealing a man's car, though," he growled, still feeling disgusted with himself. Hadn't he learned his lesson years ago? After all, Jenna wasn't the first city women to leave a Spencer male high and dry in Tyler when she ran off with another man.

"AND THEY SAY nothing ever happens in Tyler," Jenna muttered. When the insurance investigator, Joby Marks, handed her the phone receiver through the bars, Jenna stamped her bare foot on the cold tile floor of the cell in Tyler's police substation. "I can dial the number myself," she assured.

Joby merely stared at her, a thumb depressing the dial tone button, a finger poised over the push-button number pad as his tongue absently flicked out, touching at the edge of his handlebar mustache. "Anytime you're ready to make your call, Ms. Robinson."

She'd never be ready. She wanted to dial the damn phone herself. "I'm not an invalid."

"No, you're under arrest," the man returned pleasantly.

Heaving a sigh, she glared at him, wondering how things had gone so wrong this morning. Wanting to surprise Seth, she'd taken his car keys and headed for Marge's Diner, intending to get them some breakfast to share in bed. She'd been out front, waving through the windshield at Caroline Benning and Marge when the door of the Blazer was yanked open. The redheaded ogre who was now in front of her had grabbed her elbow, hauled her to the street, slammed her against the side of the sport-utility and then Mirandized her as if she were a common criminal. He hadn't even let her get her shoes, which were still on the floor mat. Even worse, all she was wearing under her leather coat was a button-down shirt of Seth's, sans underwear. Now she swallowed hard. "Just give me the phone." If nothing else, making demands restored a shred of her dignity, not that Joby Marks responded.

"This is it, huh?" called Stew Cary from his desk, sounding excited. He glanced into a small clasp envelope and jiggled the contents. "I knew she was wearing the ring. When the two of them came in here asking about you, I saw it on her finger, Joby."

Jenna glanced slowly around the cell, taking in the exposed toilet, roll of scratchy paper and hard cot. She thought she'd explode. "Look," she managed. "I'm not telling you how to do your job or anything, but that's not even a real diamond, it's a cubic zircon."

Stew Cary chuckled. "So that's your story."

"It's not a story, it's the truth," she returned, fighting her temper. Why couldn't these locals just call New York? "I know it looks real, but it's not. And it's not stolen. The ring was made by an artist named Antonio Juarez. He shows out of a gallery in Soho where I work, which is called Soho Designs. I've got the number. If you'd simply—"

"Call there?" Joby lifted a thumb from the dial-tone button long enough to drag a hand through his carrot hair. "Where do you think I've come from?"

The man *did* have a New York accent. "Not the gallery?" She couldn't believe it.

"He's from the insurance company," Stew cut in, sounding proud to be a part of this bust. Gretchen was slung around his hip, and she seemed to be enjoying herself. As Stew strode away from an open doughnut box, carrying a donut, Gretchen tried to nab a bite and got a white powder spot on her nose. "Joby's been staying with me ever since he flew into town."

"Cozy," Jenna couldn't help but say dryly. Trying not to panic, she added, "It really is a cubic zircon."

"No, ma'am," Joby corrected. "The artist always includes a real diamond in every show and as a long-term employee of the gallery, I'm sure you knew that. Don't try to play dumb." His voice lowered with insinuation. "Didn't you know that, Ms. Robinson?"

Her heart thudded against her ribs. Was it true? Had she inadvertently taken a real diamond from the gallery? "I left a note," she managed weakly.

"I was in the gallery," Joby returned.

Great. "No note?" she guessed.

"No note," he confirmed.

"Something must have happened to it," she argued, becoming increasingly worried about being stuck in this small-town substation with two blood-thirsty cops who were obviously as crazy as loons. "Do I look like a thief?" When no one answered, she added, "The gallery owners are my best friends. Sue and Dom—"

Joby Marks nodded. "I met them. The engaged couple."

"Engaged?" Her pulse beat quickened. That had to be wrong. "They're not engaged. *I'm* engaged to Dom."

At that Joby and Stew both laughed. Tweaking the long curling end of his mustache, Joby said, "Really? I take it that's why you had to *steal* an engagement ring?"

Color rose on her cheeks. She'd about had it with these two. "I didn't steal it," she bit out between clenched teeth.

Stew had the nerve to hum a few bars of the wedding march. "Anyway," he said. "For a woman whose engaged to a man in New York, it looks as if you've been having a pretty good time in Tyler, Wisconsin."

It took everything she had not to react. But she knew how she looked, with uncombed, sleep-tousled hair and a man's shirt peeking out from the collar of her coat. Not to mention the fact that she was, quite literally, barefoot and pregnant. Right then and there, she had a half a mind to simply announce that she wasn't wearing panties, just to shock these two out of their damnable complacency.

A long silence had fallen.

Joby Marks finally rolled his eyes. "Lady," he said, "do you want your phone call or not? I'm getting tired of standing here waiting to dial for you."

Jenna simply couldn't believe this was happening. "No dime for a phone call anymore, huh?"

"No, but since calls are a quarter, I guess it's your lucky day."

Lucky was the last thing she felt. While Joby was still chuckling at his own attempt at wit, she forced herself to take a deep breath and count to ten. Then she rattled off Seth's number. Pressing the receiver to her ear, she coiled the cord between her fingers and waited, praying that Seth hadn't taken his phone off the hook. Maybe he'd done so last night before he'd come to bed. "C'mon, Seth," she murmured.

But the phone rang and rang.

Chapter Twelve

"Pick up the phone," Seth muttered, his mood souring since Dom Milano was the last person he wanted to talk to right now. As much as Seth hated swallowing his pride and calling his rival, he wanted to make sure Jenna phoned him the second she got into New York. "If she's even going there, and if Dom remembers to tell her," Seth added, trying not to dwell on the potentially jealous attributes of the Italian Lothario. When had Dom become so interested in Jenna, anyway? For ages, Seth had been so sure Dom's eye was trained on Sue Ellis.

But then, what did Seth Spencer—or any of the Spencer men—know about deep, lasting attachments? Surely, after yet another woman left them for the bright lights, big city and another man, the tongues of Tyler, Wisconsin, would wag, just as they had on that long-ago Thanksgiving day when Violet Spencer had left town. Seth shook his head as if to clear it of confusion. Earlier, after he'd realized Jenna had left the house with Gretchen, he'd hesitated. He'd told himself to let her go, but of course he couldn't. Years ago, maybe his father should have followed his mother, too. Maybe the Spencer's lives would have been different.

Now he wedged the receiver of the pay phone under his jaw and listened to the endless ringing. Why wasn't Dom picking up? Glancing around the airport, Seth felt as if he was going stark raving mad. Borrowing his father's car, he'd driven straight here— only to realize he'd come on nothing more than a rush of pure impulse and adrenaline. He was moving on exactly the same mindless energy he'd used to chase the redheaded guy through the town square. Why hadn't he bothered to call ahead for flight information? Now he could only hope that the redhead hadn't really nabbed Jenna. Surely, wherever she'd gone in the Blazer, she was fine, he told himself. She was a big girl, thoroughly capable of taking care of herself. But dammit, where was she? And why had Seth been so foolishly convinced she'd headed for New York?

Because your mother did.

Jenna wasn't his mother, though. She didn't appear to be on any of the New York flights scheduled today, either. Some airlines offered connecting flights, but Jenna wasn't listed as a passenger on them. Despite his mood and the difficulty in getting the information, Seth had managed to charm an attendant, saying he was worried about his pregnant wife. Still listening to the annoying ring of Dom's phone, Seth licked against the dryness of his lips, an unsettling sense of unreality stealing over him. *She couldn't have left me.*

Not after how close we were last night…not when we're having a baby together.

And yet as he'd zipped out of Tyler, he hadn't seen hide nor hair of his Blazer. Jenna wasn't in the airport, either. There'd be no missing her. The suitcases alone would take up half the airport, not to mention the wedding dress. Was she driving his car back to New York? He wouldn't put it past her, he thought cursing softly under his breath.

"Maybe she didn't take her stuff, after all," he whispered on a sudden revelation. Maybe she wasn't even really gone. He groaned. Had she put her suitcases in his closet? He realized he hadn't even taken the time to look in the closet and see if her clothes were still there. He wasn't sure but, come to think of it, he hadn't noticed the suitcases in his bedroom last night, probably because Jenna had so thoroughly captured his attention, wearing that green silk nightie. But if she hadn't left Tyler, why had she left his house?

For the umpteenth time, he wished Jenna was a bank instead of a woman, or something else he could more easily understand, such as spreadsheets. Columns of numbers made so much more sense than emotions. And when it came to emotions, love was the worst, he decided. He'd handled stock market crashes without blinking, but the mother of his coming baby had him so tangled up that he thought he'd implode. What was he going to say if Dom ever answered the phone? Hell, he wasn't even entirely sure why he was calling Dom—except that he might know if Jenna had made any plans to go back to New York.

The phone was still ringing.

And ringing.

"C'mon," Seth muttered. As if in answer, the phone clicked as someone picked up on the other end. Seth said, "Hello? Dom?"

A woman giggled. Hearing the light, airy bubbling sound, Seth illogically thought that somehow Jenna had already managed to get to New York. Just as he realized that was impossible, he frowned, recognizing the voice. It was Sue Ellis.

"Sue?" he said.

More laughter sounded…then a cork…then a male chuckle…then a voice that said, "Dom Milano speaking."

"Sounds more like Dom Pérignon champagne," Seth couldn't help but say dryly.

Dom laughed. "Seth?"

Seth was still frowning. "Yeah."

"I knew it. I recognized your voice."

What Seth recognized was something that sounded suspiciously like creaking bed springs. Glasses clinked. Silk rustled. Straining, Seth thought he actually heard smacking kisses. It definitely sounded as if Dom and Sue were having a champagne breakfast in bed, and despite his relief that Sue, not Jenna, was in Dom's bed, Seth was strangely furious on Jenna's behalf. His voice came out dangerously flat. "Well, I can tell you two are occupied, so I won't keep you too long."

"No trouble," Dom said with a chuckle, not sounding the least bit concerned by the fact that a woman other than his fiancée was in his bed. "I'm glad to hear from you. We've missed you in New York, you know."

Seth cut to the chase, doing his best to ignore a sweet-looking elderly woman who had sidled up and was now staring at him pointedly and jingling coins, obviously eager to use one of the phones. Seth glanced toward a woman at the next booth who was winding up her conversation and said, "I don't suppose you've heard from Jenna?"

The bedsprings creaked again, and Seth assumed Dom was sitting up, punching some pillows against a headboard and making himself comfortable. "No," Dom said, sounding concerned. "We thought she was with you. She's in Tyler, right?"

"Yeah. At least she was."

"Where's Gretchen?" Sue's equally worried voice sounded in the background.

"With Jenna." Seth sighed. "Look," he couldn't help but say to Dom, "I don't want be nosy, but I was under the impression you'd proposed to Jenna."

There was a long silence.

Seth repositioned the phone under his jaw, forcing himself to shoot an apologetic smile at the woman who was waiting for the phone and feeling relieved when the woman next to him ended her call. He nodded to the elderly woman, saying, "That phone's available now."

Using a cane, the woman hobbled over and picked

up the other telephone as Dom said, "Well, actually, Sue and I are getting married."

Seth squinted. "What?" he murmured, then he listened as Dom explained the situation. "Let me get this right," Seth said after Dom finished. "You asked Jenna to marry you, but only so she'd come to Tyler and tell me about the baby? You were matchmaking?"

"She loves you, Seth," Sue said into the phone. "She's been driving Dom and me crazy. All she ever does is talk about you."

Seth could barely believe it. "She does?"

Sue and Dom laughed. Sue said, "We have regular gallery powwows about whether she should call you."

He frowned. "Whether she should call me?"

"You know," said Sue. "Whether you'll really want to hear from her, whether it's too soon to call, whether she's waited long enough since the last time she called you."

It was hard to imagine Jenna worrying over him that way, given her outward confidence. "Really?" he murmured into the receiver.

"Seth this, Seth that," Dom put in cheerfully. "I just thought she needed more confidence in her own innate lovability. I figured if she was sure she could marry me, she'd be more forceful in demanding love from where she most wanted it."

"From where?" Seth was lost.

"From you," Dom clarified.

"You two belong together," Sue assured.

Seth's spirits lifted at the words, then just as quickly plummeted. Riding an emotional downward spiral, he glanced around, feeling increasingly worried, wondering once more about the redheaded stranger who he could swear had been following Jenna. "Wherever she is."

Dom's phone beeped. "Hold on," he said. "It's call waiting. Maybe it's Jenna." Before Seth could respond, Dom had switched to the other line, leaving Seth to consider his options. Should he head back to Tyler? Or call Cooper Night Hawk from here? When it came to finding that redhead, Seth definitely wanted some action. What was wrong with the cops? "Dammit," he cursed under his breath. He shouldn't have listened to Jenna. He should have questioned the man last night at Stew Cary's house when he'd had a chance. "C'mon, Dom." Pretty soon, Seth was going to run out of quarters.

A moment later the phone clicked back on. "Sorry," Dom said. "It was the insurance investigator." He blew out a short sigh, then continued. "Look, I don't know where to start. Remember that artist Antonio Juarez?"

Seth nodded, wondering where Dom was headed with this, and what this had to do with Jenna. "Yeah."

"Well, you know how we're displaying his costume jewelry?"

Seth recalled going to Elaine's restaurant with Dom and Sue after Antonio Juarez had decided to show his work in their gallery, but now he was getting impatient. Staring through the airport windows, he realized that a meter maid was putting a ticket on his father's car. *Just my luck.* "What's Antonio Juarez's show got to do with Jenna?"

"She took a diamond from the gallery, thinking it was a cubic zircon, but it's the genuine article. Antonio always includes one real diamond in his show. Anyway, we found Jenna's note last night, and we've been trying to reach the insurance investigator ever since."

Seth couldn't really follow. "You called an insurance investigator?"

"Yeah. We had to. We thought we'd been robbed. Now I feel terrible. I guess Jenna's note must have blown off the top of the jewelry case where she left it. It's been misplaced all this time."

"*She's* misplaced," Seth muttered. "I just wish I knew where she was."

"I was getting to that," said Dom. "She's in a Tyler jail."

JENNA WAS BEING released from the jail cell when Seth strode into the Tyler substation, carrying a bouquet of roses. Unfortunately, she was too damn mad to react to the gift. "I've been trying to call you," she couldn't help but huff. Staring down at her embarrassing outfit, she grasped the ends of the leather coat's tie belt and cinched it around her waist. Not having bars between her and the rest of Tyler was serving to remind her she was barefoot and practically naked beneath the coat. Tying the belt tightly seemed to help her feel more secure, if only marginally.

Ignoring Seth, she headed toward Stew Cary just as the bars clanked shut behind her. Gretchen was still slung around the man's hips, and when the baby giggled as if finding humor in Jenna's situation, the first hint of a smile flickered over Jenna's lips.

"Sorry, ma'am," Stew murmured, a faint, sheepish flush stealing over his cheeks as Jenna self-righteously lifted Gretchen from his arms.

"You should be sorry," Jenna returned, unable to spare the man despite her usual generosity.

Stew eyed Joby Marks who defensively said, "Sorry, but I was doing my job, Ms. Robinson."

She arched an eyebrow. "Harassing citizens is your job?"

"According to all the information I had," Joby returned, "and given the fact that you were wearing a stolen diamond, I'm sure you understand my position."

Jenna could merely gape. "Do you think you were justified in arresting an innocent woman?"

"Not so innocent."

This time the speaker was Seth. Readjusting Gretchen's legs around her waist, Jenna turned toward him. "And you," she continued, not bothering to fight her pique. "I've been trying to call for an hour. I needed you." Just as she finished saying the words, something inside her calmed. She was fine, she realized. She'd been released from jail, Gretchen was in her arms again, and the man she'd shared a bed with last night was here now, looking finer than spun gold.

He said, "I was looking for you."

As her eyes drifted over him, she realized the truth of it. So much for the button-down Seth Spencer she was so accustomed to seeing. He was thrusting a hand through his usually tidy hair, smoothing it as if he'd just become aware that it was sticking up at odd angles. A wrinkled shirt was buttoned cockeyed and tucked sloppily into the trousers he'd worn yesterday, which had spent the night on the floor next to her sexiest nightie. Just seeing him in such a disheveled state unhinged her. Before she knew what was happening, her throat closed up and her mouth went dry, and no matter how hard she tried, she couldn't swallow around the lump. "Looking for me?"

He nodded, still holding the roses. "At the airport."

She shifted Gretchen in her arms. "The airport?" she said, emotion claiming her as she eyed the roses. "Why would you go there?"

"I thought you went back to New York."

Was he crazy? Why would she do that? Unable to do much more than parrot him at the moment, she said, "New York?"

He shrugged, then glanced around the substation, eyeing Stew and Joby, clearly wishing they'd vanish. Neither man took the hint; instead, they leaned against a desk, side by side, getting comfortable in order to better indulge their curiosity about what was happening between Seth and Jenna. Sighing, Seth gave up on their leaving and crossed the room.

As he neared, Jenna felt her knees weaken. Backing up and resting against the cell bars for support, she fixed her eyes on his as he stopped in front of her. Gretchen reached out, a tiny fist closing over his lapel as if to draw him even nearer.

Smiling down at the clenched hand, Seth took another step toward Jenna, bunching the roses in the crook of an arm, so both his hands were free to settle on her waist. He pulled her against him.

"You were looking for me at the airport?" she managed again, her breath catching as her eyes searched his. Last night had been so wonderful. Had he really thought she was leaving him? "Seth," she said in a rush, swallowing her pride for the first time since she'd come to Tyler, "I want to stay here. When you left New York, I was mad since you didn't ask me to come with you. I didn't even want to come here without having other reasons, such as working for Molly."

His eyes softened. "Why didn't you say anything?"

"I—I'm so tired of chasing after love," she admitted. "Can't you understand? I don't want to have to beg. I just want love to come to me. I deserve it."

His hands tightened on her waist and his voice lowered, becoming barely audible. "Oh, Jenna," he said simply. "You do deserve love. And you've got mine. You always have."

Without shoes, she was shorter than he, and now

she gazed up, peering into his eyes, her heart thudding. "I do?"

"Of course you do." Lifting a hand, he lightly brushed strands of hair from her temple, understanding in his penetrating gaze. "But you've been waiting for me to reach out, Jen, when reaching out isn't something I know how to do."

She fought it, but tears stung her eyes. Blinking them back, she whispered, "Did you want to reach out?"

"Yeah."

"Could we ever change?"

His words were husky. "I think we have already."

She felt confused. "When did we do that, Seth?"

"We're doing it right now. We're doing it this very minute."

It was a heady thought. Shifting Gretchen again, she lifted her free hand and brought it to his face, cupping his cheek. "You really think so?"

He nodded. "I didn't know it until you drove that crazy-looking Cadillac into Tyler, but my past has been ruling me, Jen. I look back on the time we spent together in New York, and I can see how I skirted you, trying to get close physically but needing to distance myself emotionally. Every time things would get too hot and heavy, I wouldn't call you for a while, or I'd bury myself in work, acting as if I had no choice but to do so. All I was feeling was love for you, though, tangled up with fear."

Her heart almost hurt. Inside her, it was stretching to the breaking point. "Fear?"

He considered a long moment. "Yeah, fear. When my mother took off and didn't keep in touch with us, something inside me closed up. Without completely realizing it, I made a pact with myself to never love anybody again, or to let anybody love me. But you started opening me back up, Jen. It's taken a long time. Little by little, something inside me has changed. And I was scared that if I loved you completely, the way I did my mother, that you'd leave."

"I won't," she whispered. "I promise."

He shook his head. "No," he whispered back. "I don't think you will, Jenna. I think you're in Tyler to stay. And anyway, my fears don't matter anymore. I love you. There's just no stopping it."

She could barely find her voice. She'd so desperately wanted this man since the first time she'd laid eyes on him. "Do you mean it, Seth? Can we try to belong to each other?"

"We already do."

He was right. There was no stopping the love they shared. "Can we raise our baby here?"

Edging closer, Seth glided a hand downward from her waist, molding it over her hip. Lowering his head, his lips sought hers, covering her mouth with more gentle tenderness than she'd ever felt. And then he whispered, "We'll raise this baby and other ones, too. We couldn't have it any other way."

Epilogue

"I can't believe this is really happening to us," Jenna whispered, her hand curling tightly over the shoulder of Seth's tux. He squeezed a hand to her waist, turning her gracefully in his arms while all of Tyler looked on.

"I can't believe it, either, Jen," Seth confessed, leaning closer to whisper the words into her ear. Warmth flooded him as he acknowledged how easily Jenna followed his lead as they danced and how perfectly their bodies moved together. "I loved you from the first moment I saw you, but I never really imagined we'd get married."

She laughed softly, pressing her cheek to his shoulder. "But we did, Seth."

"Yeah, we did."

Suddenly grinning, he thought over the flurry of activity in the past month. As usual, Jenna hadn't wasted time. Within days after he'd proposed, every last stitch of her wardrobe—not to mention the rest of her belongings—had made their way to Tyler. Already, she had plans for the few nooks and crannies in the house that she hadn't already redecorated, including the nursery, which she was painting herself. Just last week, a zebra-print sofa had appeared on the porch, complete with leopard print throw pillows.

"I've never seen you look so conservative as you do in a wedding dress," he murmured now.

"Do you like it?"

"Yeah. But not as much as the fact that you're my wife."

She smiled back at him. "I'm glad Dom and Sue could come. Not really being in love with me was the best thing Dom ever did, don't you think?"

Seth laughed. "If Dom had really taken you to the altar, I'd have stopped the wedding."

Her green eyes danced at the thought. "You promise?"

"I promise," Seth assured, thinking that things had turned out perfectly. Not only had New York friends arrived in Tyler, but Reverend Sarah had performed a beautiful service in the Tyler Fellowship Sanctuary. Now practically everyone in town was milling about the decorated fellowship hall, or piling their plates at the traditional Thanksgiving buffet before heading toward countless tables that were set up around the dance floor. Brick Bauer was deep in conversation with Cooper Night Hawk who was still apologizing profusely to Seth for not getting back to him last month. Apparently, a felon had demanded Coop's full attention, and he'd had no choice but to turn over his substation to Stew Cary, who was only in training and now working in Benton.

Suddenly, Seth caught Caroline Benning's eye, and he wondered as he often had whether she'd called him to announce Jenna's pregnancy. If she had, why had she chosen to deny it when Seth asked? Shaking his head now, he decided the young woman was definitely a mystery.

Realizing Emma Finklebaum was waving at him, Seth nodded in greeting, his mouth falling into a lopsided smile. "Quinn made sure all the ladies from Worthington House made it to the wedding."

Another chuckle escaped Jenna's lips. "Those ladies will have him sewing quilts before he knows it."

"What do you think of the quilt they gave us?"

"It's gorgeous," Jenna said warmly of the wedding gift.

The patchwork quilt was the one the women had been sewing the day Jenna drove into Tyler. "There're definitely enough of those busybodies to keep my little brother busy," Seth said with good humor, glancing at the quilters' table. Martha Bauer was cautiously picking from a plate heaped high with turkey, dressing and cranberry sauce while gossiping with Tillie Phelps and Merry Linton. Bea Ferguson and Kaitlin Rodier were wending through the crowd and making their way from the buffet table.

"Who knows," Jenna said on a smile. "Maybe you'll be a trendsetter."

He squinted. "How's that?"

"You're the first of the Spencer men to marry in a long time, Seth."

The words sobered him, and his eyes settled on the Thanksgiving buffet. Years ago, Violet Spencer had left Tyler on this holiday, and now things were coming full circle. This Thanksgiving was about union, not loss; marriage, not sorrow; the future, not the past.

Seth lowered his voice, pressing a kiss to Jenna's ear. "I hope I'm not the only Spencer male to settle down, but I can't imagine Quinn and Brady doing so."

Jenna glanced toward his brothers. "Don't be too sure," she murmured. "Love comes when you least expect it."

Seth's eyes locked with hers. "Or else it's right there all along, but you're just too scared to notice."

Her green eyes sparkled. "*You* noticed."

Seth smiled in return, a sudden rush of well-being claiming him. "Yeah," he murmured, pressing a kiss to his wife's lips. "I did notice. And you know what?"

"What?" she whispered.

"It's the best thing I ever did."

Be sure to
RETURN TO TYLER
*next month
when Harlequin American Romance
presents...*

PATCHWORK FAMILY

by

Judy Christenberry

Turn the page for a sneak peek!

Chapter One

Blood pumped through Molly Blake's body as she raced across the town square of Tyler, Wisconsin.

"You're being ridiculous!" she panted to herself as she ran, but she didn't slow down. Instead, her mind listed the reasons for panicking.

Thank God it wasn't a large town square. It wasn't a large town, for that matter. But if she'd had to run any farther, she might have collapsed.

She leaned for only half a second by the discreetly lettered brass plate that read "Trask and Spencer, Attorneys-at-law." With a prayer of hope, she drew a shuddering breath and shoved away from the red brick wall of the building and slammed back the door to the law offices.

Warmth flooded her. After all, it was winter in Wisconsin, the beginning of December. Every occupied building had its heat on full blast. And she was still wearing a knitted cap over her messy long braid, still had her navy pea jacket wrapped around her, her gloves on her hands, boots on her feet.

She shivered. The cold was coming from deep within her. From her fears. From—

"May I help you?" a pleasant woman asked.

In the almost shadowy interior of the building, Molly hadn't really seen her.

Gasping for air, Molly got out, "I need to see Mrs. Trask at once. I'm Molly Blake and it's—it's an emergency."

The secretary took in Molly's worn pea jacket over a stained sweatsuit—she'd been refinishing a wooden table she'd bought for the inn's dining room before she'd run out to do some errands and met with disaster.

With the calm precision of someone who loves routine, the woman asked, "What's the nature of your business?"

"If you'll just tell Mrs. Trask I'm here—"

"I can't do that, Ms. Blake. She's out of the office."

"What?" Molly almost screamed, unable to retain any semblance of sanity. If she didn't get help, she wouldn't be sane anyway. She'd lose everything, everything she'd worked so hard for—the Breakfast Inn Bed, her investment money... No. She had to hold it together for Sara. Nothing or no one would fail her daughter again. Sara had no one else to depend on but Molly. There had to be hope...

Just as the secretary was about to speak, a door to the left of the reception desk opened and a handsome man stepped out.

"Problem, Mrs. Allen?"

It was Quinn Spencer. Molly had heard about him. In fact, she'd met him once. At that time she'd had the distinct displeasure to hear him explain with great clarity about his on-the-go lifestyle and how he had no time in his life for children. She wanted nothing to do with Amanda Trask's partner, Quinn Spencer.

"Yes, sir," the secretary said, nodding her head like a bird considering a worm. "This lady seems a bit overheated."

"An amazing feat in this weather," the lawyer drawled, raking his eyes over Molly.

In an instant, Molly's dislike turned to hatred. How easy to be above it all with a wealthy family, a secure job, a life of—of jet-setting!

He stood before her in a very expensive navy pin-stripe suit and leather wingtips that would probably cover her food budget for half a year. His light brown hair, with just a touch of blond to suggest days spent in the tropics, had been expertly cut. Businesslike, of course, but with a touch of freedom, giving him a sophisticated air of self-determination.

She looked down at her sweatsuit and instantly felt out of place. When she jerked her gaze away, it immediately collided with his. A question resided in his hazel eyes. Or were they green?

What was wrong with her? She was about to lose her business before it even opened and she was wondering about this man's eye color!

She drew a deep breath, trying to get control of herself, and faced Mrs. Allen. "When will Mrs. Trask be available?"

Surely she had made that request in a calm, professional manner. Why was the woman hesitating?

It took a nod from the attorney for the secretary to open an appointment book. "I believe she's free on the eleventh...of January," Mrs. Trask said, looking up over the rims of her glasses.

"I can't wait that long!" Molly gasped. "It'll be too late. Please—" A hand on her arm stopped her.

"I don't believe we've met," the lawyer murmured in a calming voice. "I'm Quinn Spencer."

Molly stared at him. He wanted to get into social niceties while she was dying here?

"I'm Amanda Trask's partner," he went on. "Did you say you're a client of hers?"

"Yes," she snapped.

Before she could plead for help, he spoke to the secretary. "Mrs. Allen, if you you'll pull Mrs. Blake's file, I'll see if I can assist her—" he shot her a smile "—since her visit is an emergency."

She might not like what she knew about Quinn Spencer. She might have decided thirty seconds ago that she hated him. That he was everything she wasn't. But right now she had no choice but to proceed through the office door he held open.

If she needed his help so badly, though, why did she feel like she was about to enter the lion's den?

Tyler Brides

It happened one weekend...

Quinn and Molly Spencer are delighted to accept three bookings for their newly opened B&B, Breakfast Inn Bed, located in America's favorite hometown, Tyler, Wisconsin.

But Gina Santori is anything but thrilled to discover her best friend has tricked her into sharing a room with the man who broke her heart eight years ago....

And Delia Mayhew can hardly believe that she's gotten herself locked in the Breakfast Inn Bed basement with the sexiest man in America.

Then there's Rebecca Salter. She's turned up at the Inn in her wedding gown. Minus her groom.

Come home to Tyler for three delightful novellas by three of your favorite authors: Kristine Rolofson, Heather MacAllister and Jacqueline Diamond.

HARLEQUIN®
Makes any time special™

TEXAS CONFIDENTIAL

Penny Archer has always been the dependable and hardworking executive assistant for Texas Confidential, a secret agency of Texas lawmen. But her daring heart yearned to be the heroine of her own adventure—and to find a love that would last a lifetime.

And this time...
THE SECRETARY GETS HER MAN
by Mindy Neff

Coming in January 2001 from

◈ HARLEQUIN®

AMERICAN *Romance*

If you missed the TEXAS CONFIDENTIAL series from Harlequin Intrigue, you can place an order with our Customer Service Department.

Arriving this December from

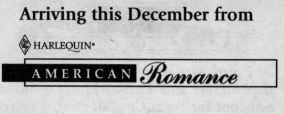

HARLEQUIN®

AMERICAN *Romance*

TWIN EXPECTATIONS
by
Kara Lennox

Identical twins Liz and Bridget Van Zandt always
dreamed of marrying and starting families at the
same time. But with their biological clocks ticking
loudly and no suitable husbands in sight, the
sisters decided it was time to take action.

Their new agenda: Have babies without
the benefit of grooms. They never expected
they'd meet two eligible bachelors whose
destinies were about to crash headlong
into their carefully laid plans....

**Don't miss the fun and excitement in this special
two-stories-in-one volume from Kara Lennox
and Harlequin AMERICAN *Romance*!**

HARLEQUIN®
Makes any time special ™

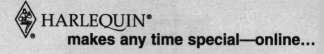

TYLER

Here's your opportunity to order the original 12 Tyler books! Each book is a self-contained story; together, they stitch the fabric of a community.

Join the residents of Tyler as they piece together the forty-year-old secret of America's favorite hometown.

#82501-3	**WHIRLWIND** by Nancy Martin	$3.99 U.S.	☐
#82502-1	**BRIGHT HOPES** by Pat Warren	$3.99 U.S.	☐
#82503-X	**WISCONSIN WEDDING** by Carla Neggers	$3.99 U.S.	☐
#82504-8	**MONKEY WRENCH** by Nancy Martin	$3.99 U.S.	☐
#82505-6	**BLAZING STAR** by Suzanne Ellison	$3.99 U.S.	☐
#82506-4	**SUNSHINE** by Pat Warren	$3.99 U.S.	☐
#82507-2	**ARROWPOINT** by Suzanne Ellison	$3.99 U.S.	☐
#82508-0	**BACHELOR'S PUZZLE** by Ginger Chambers	$3.99 U.S.	☐
#82509-9	**MILKY WAY** by Muriel Jensen	$3.99 U.S.	☐
#82510-2	**CROSSROADS** by Marisa Carroll	$3.99 U.S.	☐
#82511-0	**COURTHOUSE STEPS** by Ginger Chambers	$3.99 U.S.	☐
#82512-9	**LOVEKNOT** by Marisa Carroll	$3.99 U.S.	☐

(limited quantities available)

TOTAL AMOUNT	$ _____
POSTAGE & HANDLING	
($1.00 each book, 50¢ each additional book)	$ _____
APPLICABLE TAXES*	$ _____
TOTAL PAYABLE	$ _____
(check or money order—please do not send cash)	

To order, send the completed form, along with a check or money order for the total above, payable to **TYLER,** to: 3010 Walden Avenue, P.O. Box 9077, Buffalo, NY 14269-9077.

Name: _____

Address: _____ City: _____

State/Prov.: _____ Zip/Postal Code: _____

Account # (if applicable): _____ 075 CSAS

*New York residents remit applicable sales taxes.
NOT AVAILABLE TO CANADIAN RESIDENTS.

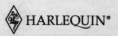

HARLEQUIN®

Visit us at www.eHarlequin.com

HARTYLBL